THE FIELDS
and the HILLS

THE FIELDS
and the HILLS

BOOK ONE
The Journey, Once Begun

by Harald Bakken

CLARION BOOKS · NEW YORK

Clarion Books
a Houghton Mifflin Company imprint
215 Park Avenue South, New York, NY 10003
Text copyright © 1992 by Harald Bakken

Map and interior decorations copyright © 1992 by David Wiesner

Book design by Carol Goldenberg.

Library of Congress Cataloging-in-Publication Data

Bakken, Harald, 1935–
The fields and the hills / by Harald Bakken.
p.   cm. — (The Journey, once begun ; bk. 1)
Summary: Journeying to the Tamish city of Domn, Weyr, a thirteen-year-old
orphan with special senses, gains self-acceptance and an awareness
of his talents as a performer when he meets an Agari family and
joins their acting and singing troupe.
ISBN 0-395-59397-2
[1. Fantasy.]   I. Title.   II. Series: Bakken, Harald, 1935–
Journey, once begun ; bk. 1.
PZ7.B1784Fi   1992
[Fic] — dc20   91-18796
                                                            CIP
                                                         AC r91

BP 10 9 8 7 6 5 4 3 2 1

TO MARJORIE

for the past and the gift of new beginnings,
for the present and the wonder of love,
for the future and the vista of endless marvelous
journeys together

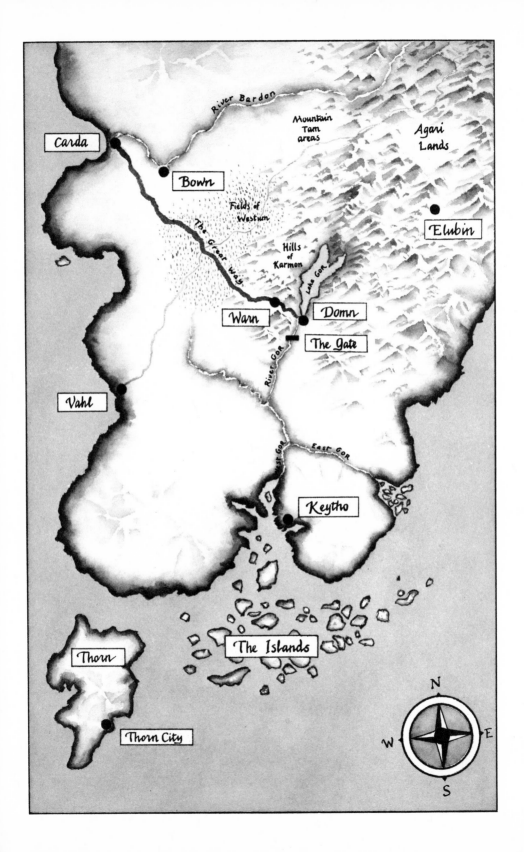

THE FIELDS
and the HILLS

Chapter One

WEYR HEARD THE adult voices talking about him. He knew he was not supposed to hear them. He knew, too, that other people would not have been able to hear them at all. The two men and the woman who would decide what to do with him — the Elders of Bown — were half a mile away in a small room in the center of the village. But Weyr heard them.

Weyr sat cross-legged on the dirt floor in one room of the two-room adobe house where he had lived with Gran. He shifted his weight. The rough wool of the borrowed chiba he had put on that afternoon for Gran's funeral rites scratched his thighs. Weyr seldom wore a robe, and he was not used to the feel of it.

The room smelled of walp. Weyr had garlanded the house with branches from the funereal plant, as custom demanded, but only because it had been expected of him. Weyr hated the acrid smell of the brittle, iron-red leaves. And he did not grieve Gran's death. Not at all.

Something brushed against Weyr's ankle. He opened

his eyes and looked down. A small salam stood motionless on its hind legs directly in front of him. Moonlight from Danger, the largest of the three moons, filtered in through an unshuttered window and glinted on the little lizard's scales. The scales were bright green. The salam would probably be a good racer. Weyr shook his head in irritation at himself. He had no time to think about that now. Weyr swatted at the lizard, and the salam scurried away.

Weyr closed his eyes against the moonlight. His extended senses were usually a little more reliable if he closed his eyes. But they were never very reliable.

Weyr had already listened for many minutes while the Elders discussed topics about which he had little interest: what it would cost to dig the new village well for Bown, what price recently birthed ab calves might bring at the Grand Market, what effect the unusually heavy late-spring rains would have on newly seeded fields. Now the Elders had begun to talk about him. He fervently hoped his hearing would not fade away. He needed to know what the Elders would say. Weyr concentrated on the voices as he heard them in his head.

"Someone has to take him in, now that old Zerbu's dead, may her spirit find its Tranquility," a female voice said. "He's too young to contract his own labor, at least here. They do say they let them contract alone that young in the Fields."

That was Anzia, who fed and housed the infrequent travelers who spent a night in Bown on their way to or from Carda. Anzia called her house the Inn.

"How old is he, ten or eleven?" a male voice said.

The male voice belonged to a man named Borno, Weyr

knew. Borno had recently returned to Bown to claim his dead father's substantial estate. In a few ninedays he had already gained a reputation as a cruel successor to a kind father.

"We reckon him at about thirteen," Anzia's voice said.

"Small for his age, then. Perhaps he has Agari blood in him," Borno said. He gave a short, harsh laugh. "Little runts, most of the Agari are. I saw some of them once in a while in Carda."

"No, he's Tam," Anzia said. Her voice had a rasp to it, as though she was forever trying to clear her throat. "Look at the width of his nose or the color of his face, and you won't have any doubts. The relief party brought him back from up north during the Great Flood. That was . . . let's see . . . the year after last Comet Turn. Seven years ago. You remember the Great Flood, Borno?"

"I heard about it."

"The boy's parents drowned," Anzia said. "And he's Tam, all right. There haven't been any Agari that far north for a generation or more."

"Unless one of them came down the river as a fish," Borno said with another harsh laugh.

"Don't say that!" a different male voice said. That was Gar, a farmer.

"I was just joking."

"You shouldn't joke about the Agari, Borno," Gar's voice said. "Some say they're witches. I never heard a story about one turning himself into a fish, though."

"Ab splatter!" Borno said. "That's back-country superstition. In Carda no one believes the Agari are witches."

"You're always talking about what they do or don't do

• 3 •

in Carda." Gar's voice was irritated. "If you thought so well of Carda, why didn't you stay there?"

"I know my duty," Borno said.

"Bicker about Carda later," Anzia said. "What are we to do with the brat?"

"What's the boy like?" Borno asked. "Besides being a runt. I took a look at him today at Zerbu's rites. He's not uncomely."

"He has a reputation as a solitary," Anzia said. "He doesn't talk much. He comes to the Inn when there are travelers, sits in a corner, and listens, quiet like. I don't think he mixes much with the other children — not that Zerbu ever left him a lot of time for that, anyway. No doubt the fact that he's not village born doesn't help him with the children. He seems bright enough, though. The boy evidently learned to read and write. He helped Zerbu with her records when her eyes began to give out."

"Will he work?"

"Zerbu said he's a hard worker," Anzia said. "But headstrong. She had to go get him a couple of times when he ran away up north, toward his birthing place. That was a while ago, though. He's been steady since."

"Not a bad investment, then," Borno said.

"Can you take him in, Gar?" Anzia asked. "You can always use another hand in your fields, even if he's something of a runt. And he has a pleasant singing voice, if you fancy entertainment of an evening. He sang once or twice at Festival. How about it, Gar?"

"No," Gar said.

"Why not?"

"My . . . my children don't like him."

"By The Comet," Borno said scornfully. "You let your children make your decisions for you?"

"My wife, too," Gar said. "They all say he sees around corners, hears things no one else can hear. Maybe he has Agari blood, after all. Agari witch blood."

Weyr felt his cheeks flush. He knew that children in Bown thought him a witch. "Weyr's a witch! Weyr's a witch!" they sometimes taunted. "Do us a witch trick, Weyr!" He had not known that adults talked that way as well.

"More back-country superstition!" Borno said. "There are no witches, Agari or otherwise."

"Still, they say it," Gar persisted. "My wife told me that once when Zerbu had taken on more wine than she should have, she said the child was a witch."

"How long was the runt with Zerbu before she died?" Borno asked.

"Four or five years, perhaps a little more," Anzia said. "Before that he was moved around wherever there was need of something a small one could do."

"Zerbu told my wife the boy started to get witchy two or three years ago," Gar said.

"Zerbu no doubt took care of that," Borno said. He gave another harsh, snorting laugh. "I remember Zerbu well, may her spirit find its Tranquility. She kept the boy in hand, I'll wager. Not much in the head, Zerbu, but she had a will like iron."

"She said she knew how to beat the witchiness out of him," Gar said.

The sound of the voices of the two men and the woman continued, but for a moment Weyr could hardly hear them for a welter of painful memories. Gran — she had insisted he call her that, not Zerbu, and he hated her for it — probably had thought that she *had* beaten the witchiness out of him. Once, when he had first begun to realize that he could see and hear, and even sometimes smell and taste, at distances no one else could, Weyr had told Gran about the sensations. She had beaten him with an ab-leather thong, screamed foul names at him, and then shut him up in an outbuilding for a whole day. Weyr had not mentioned the sensations to Gran again.

At first he had not been so cautious with the children. He had shown them what he could do, even boasted about it. He was an outsider in Bown. He knew that. He hoped that the strange abilities might make the children accept him, like him, just as they seemed to like him when he made them laugh at the way he could mimic their elders.

Gradually, Weyr had come to realize that when he showed off his unusual abilities, the children's eyes were wide not with awe or even envy, but with fear. They called him "witch" behind his back, and sometimes they called him "witch" to his face. There were fights. Weyr thought he acquitted himself well in the fights, given his small size. But he had begun to keep his own counsel about the strange sensations. After a time he had developed an inviolable rule about them. Never tell anyone. Never.

"I fail to see," Anzia was saying in her rasping voice, "why the stories of children or even of an unusually sheltered woman — begging your forgiveness, Gar, but it's true — should make it so hard to dispose of one uncontracted boy."

"Hear, hear!" Borno said.

"Let's get on with it," Anzia said. "We have more important things to discuss. If you won't take him, Gar, what do you suggest? Perhaps . . ."

"I'll take him," Borno said. His voice had a sneer to it. "I'll take him, 'witchiness' and all. He won't keep those notions long. I'm not one to fall prey to back-country superstitions. And he'll be so busy earning his keep, he won't have time for any nonsense."

"So!" Anzia said. "Gar, what do you think?"

"Borno's welcome to him," Gar said.

"An agreement, then," Anzia said. "Do you want to get him now, Borno? He's still at Zerbu's."

Weyr felt the muscles in his stomach tighten.

"In the morning," Borno said. "I have plans for certain . . . entertainment . . . tonight. He won't be going anywhere."

Weyr stopped listening to the voices. In a minute they faded away. He stood up. His head throbbed and his leg muscles were cramped. He had been sitting motionless for a long time, listening and thinking.

Weyr knew what he had to do. The thought of being a servant to Borno, as he had been so long to Gran, filled him with dread. Gran's harshness he knew. Borno's he had only heard about. And now he knew that not only the children in the village, but some adults as well, believed he was a witch. The idea of remaining in Bown with anyone seemed impossible.

Weyr moved quickly. He pulled the borrowed chiba off over his head. For a moment he considered taking the robe with him. He had never owned any formal garments.

But this one belonged to the village and was lent out only for ritual occasions, usually funerals. Others who could not afford formal clothing would need the chiba. It would not be right to take it away.

Weyr folded the robe neatly and laid it on the single table in the room. He tugged the brown linen tob he usually wore up over his legs, tied it tight with the belt, and slipped a blav over his head. The light pants and blouse were a relief after the heavy robe. He eased his feet into the ab-leather boots Gran had reluctantly bought him when he had, by her reckoning, turned twelve, old enough to be given adult footwear.

Weyr gathered the only other tob and the two other blavs he owned, a knife and some additional cooking utensils, and a few more small things he thought he might need. There was some leftover food from the funeral meal on a shelf near the hearth. Weyr took two loaves of lan, half a rind of ab-milk cheese, and a few boam leaves stuffed with three-bean wurd. With rope he tied everything into two ab-hair blankets to make a crude pack and slung it up on his back. The pack felt easy on him. He was small for his age, but strong for his size.

The food would last him for a day or so, but then he would need money. Weyr supposed he could work asham. He had done that for a short time in Bown. Most villages, he had learned from travelers at Anzia's Inn, kept common land where a man or woman — or, Weyr hoped, a boy — who was down on his luck could work for a few days, a few months or a year, or even a Comet Turn if one chose, in order to earn enough to stay alive. But it would be better if he started with a purse.

Weyr stopped before the hearth. One stone was slightly loose. Behind it, Weyr knew, Gran had kept her coins, the ones she earned from the transcribing and record keeping she did for people in the village and the ones she won in her inveterate and often shrewd betting on the salam races and other games. He eyed the stone. Gran hadn't thought he knew where she kept her money. But sometimes when his sight had extended, he had seen her put coins behind the stone.

Weyr reached toward the hearth, hesitated briefly, then shrugged and pried the stone loose. Gran was dead, drowned in the River Bardon through no fault except her own carelessness. She had no use for the money. Part of it was his money, too, though Gran had shared little of it with him. He had helped her earn it, fetching wood for her fireplace, cleaning her house, making deliveries for her, and later, after he had learned to read and write and Gran's eyesight had begun to fail, writing in the records she kept, doing her work for her.

Weyr grasped the clinking rope of coins. There was no way to tell exactly how much of the money Gran had earned and how much she had won gambling, but fair was fair, even in death. Gambling winnings were the gift of Fate. The betting money was Gran's. Weyr pulled half of the coins off the rope and tucked them back into the crevice in the hearth. He tied the rope with the remaining coins around his waist and dropped his blav over it.

Satisfied that he was ready, Weyr stepped out of the house. The warm late-spring night air smelled fresh and clean after the overpowering scent of walp inside. His headache was gone. An ab lowed somewhere in the distance. Perhaps the buffalo was calling to a newly born calf. Weyr looked up at the cloudless sky. Danger had set, but the other two moons, Dawn and Sprite, were above the horizon. There would be ample light for easy walking. Weyr was momentarily grateful that Gran's house was on the southern edge of Bown. He would not need to chance being seen by walking through the village.

The road southward out of Bown, Weyr knew, eventually angled in an easterly direction into the Fields of Westum, the enormous grain farms that made up the area travelers called "the great belly of the Tam." No doubt there were ashams there where he could work. Or perhaps he could get a regular job. Anzia had said that in the Fields people contracted for labor even with children his age. It was three or four days on foot to the Fields. He had some walking to do.

An absurd thought struck Weyr. If he really was a witch, he should be able to fly instead of walk. The witches in the stories people told to children — at least some of them — could fly. But he could not fly. All he could do was see and hear and smell in ways no one else could. If he was a witch, Weyr thought, his witchcraft was not of much use at the moment. He would have to walk, like anyone who was not a witch. Weyr snorted at the thought.

It was early in the evening. Borno would not come for him until morning. He could put a good distance between him and the village before that. Even so, Weyr doubted that anyone in Bown — not even Borno — would care enough to search for him. Who would really want to find a witch child? In any case, if they did think to look for him, they would probably assume that he had gone north, as he had when he had run away before, toward the country where he had been born. He would be able to get safely away from Bown, he was reasonably sure.

The Waterfall, the huge southern constellation, was dimly but clearly visible in the sky despite the light from the two moons. Weyr set out toward it. After a time he began to hum a song quietly to himself, and then to sing it out loud. He walked at a steady, even pace. His booted feet made a regular slapping sound on the dirt road in rhythm to the song. Weyr did not look back.

Chapter Two

WEYR STOOD AT the crossroads and tasted dust.

He had tasted dust every day for a nineday since he had started through the Fields of Westum. The wide dirt road through the Fields, called The Great Way, was clotted with travelers. They moved on foot, on horses, on abs, in horse-drawn carts, and in ab-drawn carts. All of them seemed to generate brown clouds in their wake. Dust clung to Weyr's lips, ground between his teeth when he closed his mouth, oozed into his nostrils and made them itch.

Weyr tried to spit. The meager trickle of moisture made a tiny brown spot in the dirt of The Great Way, then disappeared. He shielded his eyes with a hand against the blistering midday sun. Heat lightning flickered in the distance over gently undulating rows of grain. The fields stretched to the horizon in every direction.

A solitary bird soared far above the grain fields. Weyr thought it might be a braw, though it was hard to tell at that distance. He had seldom seen the large predatory birds in Bown. They nested, people said, in isolated spots in the mountains, and there were no mountains near Bown. But braw had great range. Weyr had seen, or thought he had seen, several above the Fields.

Closer by, Weyr spied a brown flicker of movement in a ditch beside the road. A salam, surprisingly active in the heat, slithered along the ditch. The lizard was small for a full-grown brown, perhaps six inches from blunt snout to pointed tail. Weyr saw its target: a small black crat perched silently on a sere blade of grass. The insect's short front legs and spindly antennae twitched. Abruptly Weyr heard the crat's unmistakable shrill whistle of alarm. The insect had sensed the lizard's presence. It hopped off the blade of grass and fluttered its wings. Before the insect could take to the air, the salam scurried rapidly toward it. The lizard's long tongue lashed out, and the crat was gone. The salam froze and became almost indistinguishable from the brown earth of the ditch.

Weyr blew the salam a kiss. He was not sure he really believed in salam omens, but it did no harm to be on the safe side. The day before, he had won at a salam race in one of the little villages along The Great Way by betting on a green. Perhaps he would bet on a brown like this one the next time he raced salam.

A quarter mile northward, on the road that intersected The Great Way to make the crossroads, the wagon on which Weyr had ridden for most of the morning moved slowly away from him. Brown clouds of dust spewed up from its wooden wheels and partially obscured Weyr's view of the farmer who slumped atop the wagon and the stolid, huge, gray ab that pulled it. Weyr had ridden on several such wagons during the past few days. The farmer had been quiet, incurious. He had asked no questions about why Weyr might want to travel alone through the Fields of Westum. When Weyr had requested a ride, the farmer had merely motioned him up atop the sacks that littered the wagon, grunted to the ab, and moved on.

About that, the farmer had been like most of the people Weyr had encountered during the time he had traveled through the Fields. In Bown a solitary traveler his age would have attracted attention. In the Fields of Westum, he was merely one of many men, women, and children who moved from place to place during the growing season, worked perhaps for a day or two in the Fields, and then went on. He was younger than most, but not so young that he attracted undue attention.

Weyr had had no trouble finding temporary work. On his first day in the Fields, he had sought out an asham and made the traditional request for a bed and food in return for labor on common village property. His request had been granted, but, he had learned, it had been thought peculiar. Only a half dozen Dedicates who had long-term commitments to the asham, two low-level criminals, and three or four villagers fulfilling their tithe time worked there. Able-bodied wayfarers and local people down on their luck could find more gainful employment with any of the local farmers. Later, when Weyr felt he needed work, he had looked for someone who wanted day labor. The day jobs and one or two lucky — or, Weyr liked to think, shrewd — bets on salam races had kept his money belt as filled as it had been when he had left Bown.

Still, he had been lonely. His contacts with people were

transient and casual. Weyr had not thought he would miss Bown. There was certainly no one from there he ever wanted to see again. But he did miss the familiarity of the village, the sight of the buildings, the smell of the orchards and fields, the sounds of voices he knew, even the dark contours of the house he had shared with Gran. The hot, dusty Fields of Westum were nothing like the rolling, green valley of the River Bardon near Bown.

Abruptly, through the dust in his mouth and nostrils, Weyr smelled flowers. He tasted fruit. The smell was cloyingly sweet, the taste slightly tart. Both were strange, unlike any smells or tastes he had known before. Startled, Weyr looked around him, but there were no flowers in the flowing grain fields. He had not eaten since morning. The scent and taste obviously came from his extended senses.

Weyr tried to follow the taste and smell to their source. He could not. That, too, was strange. Usually when his senses extended, he could locate the source of a sound or a sight. He almost always knew exactly where it came from, how far away it was. But these sensations came from no particular spot.

They did come from a direction. Without understanding quite how he knew it, Weyr was sure the odd smell and taste came from somewhere to the south. There was no more specific feel to it than that. They came from the south.

The strange scent and taste disappeared as abruptly as they had come. Dust clogged Weyr's mouth and nostrils again.

Weyr shook his head. Why had these sensations come to him? They had to have a meaning. An omen. Perhaps, like the salam he had seen, they were an omen. If so, what did the omen mean? The sensations came from the south. What lay to the south?

Weyr struggled to remember the little he knew about geography. He, himself, had been brought to Bown from the north, though he could remember nothing from the time before Bown except the rushing, thundering torrents of water he now knew were the Great Flood, and the screaming, awful voices he believed had been those of his parents. Weyr shivered and pushed those memories from his mind. What did he know about the south?

There were cities to the south. Wayfarers he had met had talked about them. One was called Domn. That seemed to be the most distant city any of the travelers had reached. Domn lay somewhere to the southeast. The most expansive of the travelers occasionally talked of Keytho, the great seaport city of the Tam, though none of them claimed to have visited it. Keytho, too, lay southward, but much farther south than Domn.

Very well. He would take the sensations as an omen. Until now he had been merely wandering aimlessly in the Fields of Westum, glad to be quit of Bown. Now he would go south. He would travel at least to Domn, perhaps even to Keytho, if that was necessary, to find the meaning of the omen. Weyr smiled to himself. Even if the sensations were not actually an omen, at least now he had a purpose, a definite destination. That felt good.

Weyr squared his shoulders, chose the southward road from the intersection, and began once more to walk. After a time he hummed a song to himself.

~

Weyr began to sense the sounds of the next village long before he reached it. Metal rang on metal. A smith's hammer, Weyr knew. Yelping punctuated an agitated gabble. A dog chasing geese. Wood creaked. Wood thunked against stone. Someone drawing water from a well. An ab bellowed. An owner was trying to make a recalcitrant buffalo move. They were familiar sounds, sounds Weyr had heard almost every day of his life. They made him think again about Bown.

Voices emerged from the sounds.

"That party of Agari," said an anxious, crotchety elderly woman's voice, "how long will they stay?"

"Only overnight, I imagine, si'be," said a younger, tenor male voice. "The same as they did a while ago when they came through from the other direction on their way to Carda."

"By The Comet! What were they doing in Carda?" the female voice said. "I've never heard of Agari going that far northwest."

"Who knows?"

"They should go back behind their mountains to their filthy dwarfs who mine for them and their kidnapped witch children," the woman's voice said.

"Superstitions," the male voice said. "They are people like us, the Agari."

"Monsters. Butchers."

"They have right of passage. Tam are at peace with Agari. We have been since before I was born," the man said.

"You're too young to remember, you silly calf," the old woman said. "You didn't hear the stories of the wars. They went on for a Comet Turn or more. Butchers, the Agari were. They killed Tam like crats in a cage."

"That's long past, si'be. Now the Agari fight only among themselves. Or so folks say," the man said. "They come among the Tam to trade. People tell there's a whole colony of Agari in Domn."

"Then let them stay in Domn. What are the Agari doing this far from there?"

"I don't know. They'll be gone tomorrow, I'm sure."

"And good riddance."

The voices faded. Weyr heard only the slap of his boots on the road and the occasional whistle of a crat.

Weyr shook his head in irritation. He had wanted to hear more about the Agari. Somehow, he thought, they might have something to do with him. Gran had often used the Agari name against him. One of her favorite scourges when she was angry was to call him an "Agari whelp."

Weyr snorted. What Gran had said might be just so much ab splatter. He speeded up his pace. There was one way to discover who was right about him and the Agari. A group of Agari were in the next village, and he would reach the village before sundown. He could find out something about them himself. "They are people like us, the Agari," the male voice in the village had said. That seemed reasonable, Weyr thought. The knot in his stomach warned him that not all of him felt that way. Still, whatever the Agari were like, Weyr knew he would not be content until he had at least seen them. It could do no harm to look.

~

The knot was still in Weyr's stomach as he peered down at the Agari camp. A brief conversation with two children in the village had told him where it was. Weyr crouched atop a small knoll, well hidden, he hoped, by a thick row of shrubs. The Agari were below him.

The encampment spread along the bank of a pond near The Great Way just outside the village. In some ways it looked like a gathering of traveling Tam who preferred not to use the asham or the village inns. Weyr had passed several camps of that kind in the Fields of Westum. But there were differences.

For one thing, the only animals in the camp were horses. There were no abs. Twenty-five or thirty unteth-ered horses grazed in a grassy area a hundred yards or so away from Weyr. These Agari must be wealthy if they could afford so many horses. Two short, stocky men stood among them, grooming one of the animals. Closer to Weyr, beside the pond, there were four wagons and three tents, two large and one smaller. There were elaborate geometrical patterns woven into the fabric of the smaller one. Sunlight made the tents glint gold and red and blue. The colors were dazzling, quite the opposite of the dull brown or gray of the tents Weyr had seen Tam travelers use.

Perhaps twenty men moved between the tents and the wagons or reclined near two cooking fires. Those men were small, too. Most of them wore swords. They were obviously guards of some sort. Weyr had seen armed guards with Tamish caravans on The Great Way, though never as many as this. And something else was different. Tamish guards were usually both men and women. As far as Weyr could tell, these were all men. Voices drifted up toward Weyr. The voices were loud, the sound of the language musical and rhythmic. Weyr could not understand a word of it.

The men were all pink skinned. Two of them had rufous hair. The others had shoulder-length hair of varying shades of blond. They wore loose-fitting trousers tied at the ankles and open-necked shirts tucked in at the waist. The shirts and trousers were all brightly colored, like the tents. There were reds and blues and yellows and greens and even one or two shades of pink. Weyr glanced down at his brown, rough-woven linen tob and blav. No Tam Weyr had ever seen wore such startling colors, even on Festival days.

Just below Weyr, at some distance from the colorful tents, was another wagon. A single horse grazed near it. Multicolored cloth formed an arch over the wagon. A powerfully built man — tall even by Tam standards — and a somewhat shorter woman stood near another cooking fire. The man wore a brilliant green shirt and pale-green trousers. The woman's clothes looked more like the clothing Tam usually wore. She was dressed in a dull brown tob and blav like those Weyr had on. In fact, Weyr thought, altogether the woman looked very much like a Tam. Her skin was brown, her nose broad, and her hair, which was tied up in a bun, was black. The man's skin was an intermediate shade, neither as brown as the woman's nor as light as that of the men near the tents. His shoulder-length hair was blond.

Weyr heard a high-pitched giggle. A slightly built brown-skinned girl of six or seven with braided blond hair crouched near the pond. Like the woman, she seemed to be dressed in Tamish clothes. The little girl lifted what was for her a fair sized rock, hefted it for a moment, threw it into the water, pointed at the splash it made, and giggled. Another rock. Another splash. Another giggle. The man and the woman near the covered wagon seemed to pay her no attention.

The child moved toward a large boulder. For no reason he could understand, Weyr's senses extended. He closed his eyes. In his mind he saw the girl as though she was standing next to him. Her pale-blue eyes sparkled. Weyr saw her reach for a rock near the boulder. Between the rock and the boulder Weyr saw a short, cylindrical flicker of brown and green.

"No!" Weyr screamed. "No! No! Don't touch that rock. Get away!"

Without thought, Weyr slipped his pack from his shoulders, scrambled out from behind the shrubs, and ran down the knoll toward the girl, still screaming at her. The child started, looked up at him with wide blue eyes, and cried out.

Weyr reached the child. Her hand was still stretched toward the rock. Weyr pushed her away. She fell backward into the water. With one motion Weyr snatched a dead branch from atop the boulder, kicked aside the rock toward which the child had been reaching, and beat down again and again with the branch.

The snake lay on the ground beside the rock, its green-and-brown head mashed flat and oozing yellow fluid. The tail twitched once and was still. Weyr opened his eyes. He had kept them tightly closed as he ran down the hill, he realized. His senses returned to normal. Weyr clutched the branch in his hand, breathing hard.

"Ho, you there!" said a resonant bass voice behind him, in Tam. "Who are you? And what did you do to my daughter?"

Weyr turned. The man he had seen standing beside the wagon rushed toward him. He looked enormous, with shoulders almost twice the width of Weyr's and hands the size of small shovels. Long blond hair streamed back from his head.

Weyr dropped the branch and began to run. He took only a few quick, short steps before he felt huge hands grip him by the shoulders, spin him around, and pick him up as though he weighed no more than the slight child who sat, wet, wide-eyed, and sobbing, in the shallow water of the pond.

Chapter Three

"LET ME GO! Put me down! Let me go!" Weyr shouted.

The man's huge hands gripped Weyr under his armpits and held him suspended a few inches above the ground. Weyr flailed at the man's chest. He could not reach it. His fists hit only hard, heavily muscled arms.

"Put me down!" Weyr repeated.

He felt his feet touch the ground. The man's hands slid around Weyr's shoulders, pinning his arms to his sides.

"Who are you? Where did you come from? Why did you hurt my daughter?"

The man's voice growled. Bright blue eyes glinted at Weyr from beneath brown, shaggy eyebrows. The powerful hands bit into Weyr's flesh.

"Didn't mean to hurt your daughter," Weyr said. He was trembling. "She was . . ."

"She's all right, Nomer," said a woman's voice, deep and throaty. "Berth's all right. She's just scared. And wet."

The brown-skinned woman Weyr had seen near the

covered wagon knelt by the water, the girl clutched in her arms. The child had stopped crying. The man who held Weyr turned to look at the woman and child but did not let him go.

"Answer me," the man said. He leaned his face back close to Weyr's. "Why did you . . ."

"There was a snake . . ." Weyr began.

"Breath of Life!" the woman said. "Look, Nomer! Look there. It's a flathead."

The woman pointed at the dead snake beside the boulder.

"Sweet Breath of Life!" the man said. "Sweet, sweet Breath of Life. It is. I've never seen a flathead this far into the Fields."

"It was behind the rock your . . . your daughter . . . was going to pick up," Weyr said. "I saw it and . . ."

"You killed it," the man said. He drew in a sharp breath. "The snake could have struck Berth. You frightened her away and killed it."

"Yes."

"Where were you?"

"Up there. On top of the hill, in those bushes," Weyr said. He jerked his head toward his hiding place. "I saw it from up there."

The man looked toward the bushes.

"That's a good fifty or sixty yards away," the man said. "How could you see it?"

"I have sharp eyes," Weyr said. "They say I have very sharp eyes."

"Sharp eyes, indeed, if you can see a flathead no more

than six inches long at that distance," the man said. "What were you doing up there?"

"Looking. Just looking," Weyr said. "Let me go. Please let me go."

"Looking at us?" the man said.

"Yes."

To Weyr's astonishment, the man laughed. It was a large, rippling laugh that seemed to come from deep in his broad chest. The green cloth of his shirt fluttered. The man released his grip on Weyr's shoulders.

"Looking at the Agari," the man said. His voice sounded teasing. "Spying on the foreigners, eh? No doubt you were looking for monsters, for beasts, for kidnappers? Possibly even for witches?"

"I was just looking," Weyr said. The man's tone made him feel foolish. "Just looking."

Weyr rubbed his shoulders where the man had held him. He should run, he thought. But the man was much bigger than he was. If he ran, the man could catch him easily. More, something in the man's laughter had relaxed him, reassured him.

"Nothing wrong with looking," the man said. "Though I doubt there's much interesting to see."

"May I go now?" Weyr said. "I should go."

"Yes, of course you may go," the man said. "But I hope you won't. You probably saved my daughter's life. We owe you a debt. We were preparing food. Will you eat something with us?"

"I shouldn't. I can't. I have to get back to my family," Weyr lied.

"As you wish."

Still rubbing his shoulders, Weyr walked up the hill to the shrubs. He picked up his pack, slung it upon his back, and turned to look behind him. The man, the woman, and the child stood together at the bottom of the hill. The man and woman waved at him. After a moment the little girl waved too.

Curiosity piqued Weyr again. He had come to see the Agari. These people were probably Agari, though they looked more Tamish than he had thought Agari would. Whatever they looked like, they were with the Agari party. The Agari were, perhaps, witches, though the man had made fun of the idea. The man had hospitably offered him food in gratitude for the help he had given. What harm could possibly come from eating with these people?

If Gran were still alive and had even an inkling of what he had done, or of what he was thinking, she would beat him until he cried out, Weyr knew. The thought made up his mind. Weyr walked back down the hill.

"I'd like to eat with you, si'be," Weyr said. "If I may."

"We'd be honored," the man said. A wide smile lit up his blue eyes and creased his pale face. Weyr guessed him to be in his early thirties. The smile made him look younger. "I'm Nomer."

Nomer held out his hand to Weyr. Weyr blinked in surprise. Adults shook hands when they met one another, but they seldom greeted children that way. At least Tamish adults seldom did. Weyr did not know about the Agari. He took Nomer's hand. His fingers barely reached past the middle of the man's palm.

"Si'be Nomer," Weyr said. "My name is Weyr."

"Weyr. This is my wife, Relinda," Nomer said.

Nomer's arm made a fluid movement as he gestured toward the woman. Relinda was, in fact, quite tall, though beside Nomer she seemed almost tiny. She looked lithe and muscular. She was, Weyr thought, perhaps a few years younger than Nomer.

"Si'be Relinda," Weyr said. He bowed slightly from the waist.

Relinda took two graceful steps toward Weyr, gripped his hand in both of hers, and shook it vigorously. She smiled. Her teeth were sparkling white and perfectly formed. The woman's face was radiant, Weyr thought. She was beautiful.

"Just 'Nomer' and 'Relinda' will do, Weyr," Relinda said. Her low voice was warm. "I hardly think we need be so formal after what you've done for us. We're most grateful to you."

"This is our daughter, Berthin," Nomer said. "Berth, this is Weyr."

Weyr nodded his head in greeting toward the little girl. She smiled shyly.

"Hello, Berthin," Weyr said.

The girl said something in the language Weyr had heard the armed guards use earlier. He heard his name among her words.

"I beg your pardon?" Weyr said.

"Speak Tam, Berth," Relinda said. "Weyr only understands Tam."

"Weyr has very sharp eyes," the little girl, Berthin, said in Tam.

~

Weyr took two bites of the meat-and-vegetable stew that Nomer ladled onto his plate, and tasted fire. His mouth burned and his nostrils felt as though he had inhaled smoke. Tears welled at the corners of his eyes. Weyr let out a hiss of breath, set down his plate and spoon, and took a long pull at the metal tankard of water that sat on the ground next to him. The water did not quench the fire.

"The food's a little warm for you, Weyr?" Nomer said. He chuckled. Like his laughter, his chuckle seemed to come from deep in his chest.

"You should have warned him, Nomer," Relinda said.

"Timid Tamish taste, eh?" Nomer said. He chuckled again. "I'd forgotten."

Weyr heard Berthin laugh. The little girl spooned food into her mouth, apparently unaffected by the spices that made tears trickle down Weyr's cheeks. Weyr lifted the water tankard again.

"No, no, Weyr," Nomer said. "Don't drink more. That'll only make it worse. Water spreads the spices around your mouth. Here, eat some flota. That'll absorb a little of it."

Nomer held out a circular, flat biscuit. As big around as Weyr's clenched fist, the biscuit took up only the space between the tips and second knuckles of Nomer's fingers. Weyr bit into the biscuit. It was flaky and tasted bland, almost cool.

"Move the flota around in your mouth for a minute or two before you swallow, Weyr," Relinda said.

Weyr complied. He took another bite of the biscuit. And another. The fire in his mouth subsided some.

"I'm very sorry," Weyr said. He wiped tears from his cheeks with the sleeve of his blav. Embarrassment made his cheeks feel hot, like his mouth. "I'm not used to . . ."

"Don't apologize," Relinda said. "Nomer should have warned you. He knows how long it took me to get used to Agari cooking. They call it 'Agari Fire.' Try eating it in small bites with lots of flota in between."

"At that, you did better than Rel did the first time she tasted real Agari food," Nomer said. His voice was teasing. "She nearly drowned herself trying to drink. And she still likes it only half spiced, like this."

"Half spiced, indeed, my Agari barbarian," Relinda said, teasing back. Her voice was richer and deeper than any woman's voice Weyr had ever heard.

"My timid Tam," Nomer said.

Nomer and Relinda bantered more about spices and food. Weyr ate. By taking small bites of the stew — Nomer had called it tofer, though Agari Fire seemed a better name — and then large bites of the biscuits called flota, Weyr managed to finish the food on his plate. He refused Nomer's offer of a second helping.

"Here's fruit," Relinda said. She laid a clay bowl of plums on the ground between them. "That, at least, is to Tamish tastes. I should know."

Weyr bit into a reddish-brown plum. The familiar flavor was reassuring, though Weyr could still sense the residue of the stew in his mouth and nostrils. The plum was slightly tart. It reminded him for an instant of the tang of the fruit from the south he had sensed earlier in the day.

"You know about Tamish tastes?" Weyr said cautiously.

"I should. I'm Tam," Relinda said. She smoothed back a strand of her black hair. "From near Domn."

"Then why are you . . ." Weyr bit back the rest of his sentence.

"Married to an Agari?" Relinda said.

"Yes. I'm sorry."

"No need to be. It's common enough around Domn," Relinda said. "Not that there aren't some who grumble about it, even there. It's not common around here, I know."

"You're the first Agari I've ever seen," Weyr said. "Nomer is, I mean."

"And now you can tell your family you've met a real Agari barbarian," Nomer said. The chuckle returned. "Also that you've tasted Agari Fire. And that you've lived to tell the tale."

"Nomer!" Relinda said.

Nomer was teasing him again, Weyr knew. Without thinking, he responded in kind.

"If I told them what Agari Fire was really like, people would call me a liar," Weyr said. "No one would believe me."

Nomer laughed. "More Agari monstrousness," he said.

Nomer squinted at the sun, now red against the horizon on the opposite side of the pond. He put his huge hands together, palms out, stretched his arms full length, and flexed his powerful shoulders.

"It's getting late," Nomer said. "Perhaps your family will be wondering where you are."

"I suppose they will," Weyr said.

Weyr stopped, uncertain of what else to say. He felt more comfortable with these people than he had with anyone he had met so far in the Fields of Westum, he realized. He did not want to leave them. Nomer and Relinda were silent for a moment. Berthin took a bite from a plum. Red juice squirted out of the fruit.

"You're not with family," Nomer said at last. His voice was flat, matter-of-fact. "You're traveling alone."

"Yes," Weyr said. "How did you know?"

"A hunch," Nomer said. "Just a hunch."

"It's witchcraft," Berthin said. Plum juice had coated her lips red. It dripped over her chin. "Nomer's a witch. He knows all kinds of things about people. And he does witchy tricks."

Weyr's skin tingled.

"Hush, Berth," Relinda said. "Tam don't like such joking."

"It's not a joke," Berthin said. She looked directly at Weyr and giggled. "My daddy really is a witch."

Weyr hesitated, again uncertain about what to say. He was not sure whether he should be afraid or amused. But it was hard to be afraid because of something said by a little girl with plum juice dribbling down her chin.

"Do hush, Berth," Nomer said gently. "I'm not a witch, Weyr, no matter what you may have heard your people say about the Agari. I'm just a magician, when I have to be. A conjurer. You've seen magicians perform?"

Weyr nodded. He had seen traveling magicians do their tricks among the stalls at the Grand Market. And a few times when Gran, in a rare burst of generosity, had taken him to see a play at a theatre near the Market, there had been a magician who performed before the play began.

"Where are you going, Weyr, if you don't mind my asking?" Nomer said.

"To Domn. My gran died. I've got a cousin she told me to go to if anything happened to her. He lives in Domn," Weyr said.

"We're going to Domn, too," Berthin said. "Nomer and Relinda are going to be witches there."

"Not witches, Berth," Nomer said. "Actors."

"There are those who think it's the same thing," Relinda said in a dry tone.

Nomer was silent for a moment, as though he was considering something. He looked at Relinda, who nodded slightly, and then back at Weyr.

"You're welcome to come along to Domn with us, Weyr," Nomer said. There was no teasing in his voice now. A pained expression crossed his face and was gone. "Traveling alone, especially when you're young, isn't always pleasant. I remember."

"It must be scary, being all alone," Berthin said.

"It's not so bad. I get along," Weyr said.

"I'm sure you do," Nomer said. "You don't have to make up your mind now. Stay with us this evening if you like. We'll be leaving in the morning. You can decide then."

"Thank you," Weyr said. "It's very kind of you to offer."

He was temporizing, Weyr thought.

"If you do join us, I'm afraid you'll have to put up with Agari Fire," Nomer said. His voice was teasing again.

Weyr hesitated a moment longer. But he knew he had already made up his mind.

"I guess I can manage that," Weyr said. "I'd like to go with you to Domn."

"Good," Nomer said.

"But I'm afraid you'll have to put up with a timid Tamish taste," Weyr said.

"We'll manage that," Nomer said.

~

As Weyr laid out his bedroll near Nomer and Relinda's wagon, Berthin came over to him. She smiled. Her teeth were perfectly formed, like her mother's, Weyr saw.

"It's a good thing you're going along with us to Domn," Berthin said.

"Why is that?" Weyr said.

"Because you're very brave."

"I am?"

"You saved my life when you killed that snake," Berthin said. "That was very brave. And you have sharp eyes. So you can help protect us while we're traveling."

"I don't know about that," Weyr said.

"I do," Berthin said. Her pale-blue eyes flashed. "I know lots of things."

"I'm sure you do," Weyr said.

"Anyway," Berthin said, "thank you for what you did."

~

The eight stars that made up the outline of the Waterfall shone bright in the southern sky. Only Sprite, the dimmest of the three moons, was still above the horizon. Weyr had wrapped himself in his ab-hair blankets against the slight chill that sometimes came in the evenings after the oppressively hot days in the Fields of Westum. The dust of the Fields had settled some. The air smelled clean and fresh. Weyr looked at the constellation for a time, then turned

away. Near him Nomer and Relinda were curled up together under a blanket. Next to them Berthin lay on her
back, her blanket covering only the legs of her tob. She
snored softly. Farther down the bank of the pond, Weyr
saw the three Agari tents, dim silhouettes in Sprite's light.

He had not only seen the Agari, Weyr thought, he was
among them. The slight aftertaste of the spicy stew would
have reminded him of that, if nothing else had. More than
that, he was going to travel to Domn with Agari. If, as
some Tam believed, the spirits of the dead occasionally
watched the living, Gran's spirit must be writhing. Weyr
found the idea deeply satisfying. He dropped off to sleep
thinking about it.

Chapter Four

WEYR WOKE TO the sound of music. A bass voice sang a rollicking song. For a few seconds Weyr was not sure whether he heard the song with his ears or his extended senses. The song had a complicated rhythm that sounded strange to Weyr's ear. Its melody was at once melancholy and wild. Weyr could not understand any of the words. Still half asleep, Weyr remembered dimly that he had heard the language of the song the night before.

Agari. The language was Agari. Weyr snapped awake. Nomer emerged from a wooded area up a hill. He was singing in Agari. His singing voice was as deep and resonant as his laugh. Nomer carried an armload of wood. The cooking fire, Weyr saw, already burned near the wagon. Relinda and Berthin squatted near the fire.

"Ho, sleepy," Nomer said. He dropped the wood beside the fire. "For a timid Tam who just spent his first night in the company of Agari, you seem to have slept pretty well. No monsters or witches?"

"Nomer, don't tease," Relinda said. She stirred a pot on

the fire and dropped brown powder into it. A bitter smell wafted up from the pot.

"I slept fine," Weyr said. He stifled a yawn. There was the tinge of an odd flavor in his mouth. "I can still taste the tofer a little, though."

"There's an Agari proverb about that," Nomer said. "'Anything worth tasting is worth tasting many times.'"

Weyr made a wry face.

"You'd best get up," Nomer said. "The Instrument's party will be moving on before too long. We have to be ready to leave with them."

"The Instrument?" Weyr said.

Weyr rolled out of his blankets and sat up. He had slept fully clothed. A green salam skittered out of a blanket. The lizard had probably spent the night there.

"The Instrument. The Honorable Lakren, Representative and Instrument in Domn of the Merchants of Elubin. And of assorted other Agari interests," Nomer said in a dry tone. He pointed to the Agari tents Weyr had seen the evening before. "That's the Instrument's party down there. He's the one in blue beside the smaller tent."

The three Agari tents shone multicolored in the bright morning sunlight. The short, pink-skinned armed guards Weyr had seen the night before moved between the tents. In front of the smaller tent, a man dressed in light-blue trousers and a brilliant darker-blue shirt pointed at one of the guards. Like the guards he was small. At this distance, Weyr could make out nothing about him except his size and the color of his clothing. Weyr tried to extend his senses for a better look. Nothing happened.

"That's the real Agari party," Nomer said. "We're just hangers-on. A polite afterthought."

"Have you been with them long?" Weyr said. He stood and stretched.

"We've come with them from Carda," Nomer said.

"What were they doing in Carda?" Weyr asked.

The old woman in the village had demanded an answer to the same question the day before, Weyr remembered. He wondered if he should have asked. But Nomer did not seem upset by the question.

"I don't know and I don't want to know," Nomer said. "Conducting negotiations about trade with merchants in Carda, perhaps. Rel and I try to stay clear of matters of trade. And of politics, which generally follows trade. Particularly politics. And particularly these days. The times are troubled. It's safer that way."

Nomer's answer made no sense to Weyr, but he felt reluctant to ask him to explain.

"But you are traveling with the . . . what did you call him?"

· "The Instrument. And yes, we're traveling with him."

"He has an awfully long title," Weyr said. "Is he important, the Instrument?"

"He is. Particularly in Domn, where he has his headquarters. And in the territories around Domn, too. In that whole area the Instrument is the leading figure among the Agari. He's forever on the move from town to town negotiating commercial agreements, settling disputes among merchants, and so on, generally seeing to it that the channels of trade between Tam and Agari flow smoothly. Out here he's not as well known, and there are those who take a dim view of the Agari, so he travels with quite an entourage, as you can see. Probably a wise precaution, that."

"He's going to Domn, too?" Weyr said.

"Yes. And for the moment, at least, we're part of his entourage. The Instrument has seen fit to take us under his protection. Which is not necessarily a bad thing," Nomer said. He shrugged as though to dismiss the subject.

"Breakfast coming up in a minute," Relinda announced.

Weyr rolled up his belongings in his blankets and tied them back together to make a pack. It was an hour or so after sunrise. The air was still cool, but there was already a hint in it of the heat to come.

Breakfast was more of the flat biscuits called flota. Relinda produced the hot biscuits from a small reflecting oven beside the cooking fire, put several on a plate for Weyr, and ladled warm honey over them. Weyr ate eagerly. When he had finished, he licked his fingers and took a plum from the bowl Nomer passed to him.

"No Agari Fire?" Weyr said.

Berthin, who sat near Weyr, laughed.

"Not in the morning," Nomer said. "In the morning most Agari have tastes as timid as Tam."

"Or as sensible," Relinda said. "Weyr, would you like to try some hamar?"

Relinda held out a steaming crockery mug filled with black liquid. The liquid had a powerful, bitter smell.

"What is it?" Weyr said.

"Hamar. It's made from the bark of the hamar tree,"

Relinda said. "Most Agari drink it in the morning. They say that if hamar doesn't open your eyes, nothing will. If you'd prefer, I think I have some felln somewhere."

Weyr had drunk the sweetened herb tea called felln every morning since he could remember. He had never been enthusiastic about it, at least when it was made by the recipe Gran used.

"I'll try this," Weyr said. "What's it called again?"

"Hamar," Relinda said.

The hamar tasted as bitter as it smelled. Its taste reminded Weyr of the medicine Gran had given him when he was much younger and complained of stomachaches. Unlike other children in Bown, he had always liked that flavor and had contrived to get more of the medicine. This drink also tasted good to him. And he could understand Relinda's comment about the beverage's wakeup qualities. A few sips of the liquid made Weyr feel much more alert. He drank all the hamar.

"Weyr, I imagine you'll want to meditate," Relinda said as Weyr set down the empty mug. "We have enough time, I think, if you do a brev and not an extend."

Weyr felt blood rush to his cheeks. Most Tam meditated at least once a day. Even Gran, no matter how hard she had worked him, had made him do that. He had meditated only once since he had left Bown. Perhaps that had been another way to spite Gran's memory.

"I should," Weyr said. He glanced at Nomer. "Do Agari meditate, too?"

"Not most of them," Relinda said. "I've gotten Nomer to do it, though he's not as regular as he should be. We all did a brev when we got up, even Berth."

"I find that meditation clears the mind," Nomer said. "A good Tamish custom, that."

"I should have done it before I ate," Weyr said, embarrassed again. Meditating on a full stomach was, while not exactly forbidden, not considered quite proper, either.

"Better after eating than not at all," Relinda said. "I'm still Tam enough to believe that. There are some nice spots in the woods up the hill there. Nomer and I found several this morning."

~

Weyr chose a small grassy clearing in the woods on a knoll not far from the place where he had first hidden to watch the Agari. Below him he could see the pond and the camp. One of the Agari tents had already been taken down. Two guards were folding it into a neat package. Beyond the pond there was already a thin haze of dust. Nearby a crat whistled. Weyr sat down, cross-legged, in the clearing.

Weyr consciously relaxed his body, beginning with the tips of his toes, his feet, his lower legs. He let his fingers go limp, felt the muscles in his arms relax. He slowed his breathing. In his mind he began to chant his word — not the one Gran had given him, but the one he had made up himself — and timed his breathing to the chant.

Random pictures came to him. The hearth in Gran's house in Bown. The bridge over the Bardon from which Gran had accidentally fallen to her death. The ab-drawn cart on which the farmer had given him a ride the day before. The brown salam in the ditch beside The Great Way. Berthin's lips, stained red from plum juice. Weyr did not try to empty his mind of the pictures, but he did not concentrate on them, either. The pictures came less frequently. Weyr drifted, his mind almost blank. Now and then he was aware of his breathing and of the sound of his voice as he chanted his word.

A new picture began to grow in Weyr's mind. At the edge of his consciousness, Weyr realized that it was a picture of something he had never seen before. He was in a clearing in a woods, but it was not the clearing where he had sat down to meditate. Trees with huge heart-shaped green leaves thick on their branches surrounded him. Sunlight filtered through the greenery. The leaves were not one shade of green, Weyr saw, but several, each shade subtly blending into the one next to it. Delicate flowers, pale white with pink at their centers, hung from some of the tree branches. On other branches there were clusters of oval yellow fruits the size of Weyr's hand, three or four fruits to a cluster.

Sounds and smells came. The predominant smell was sweet, almost syrupy. The odor came from the flowers. Dimly, Weyr remembered that he had smelled the scent before. Insects buzzed, though they did not make noises like any insect Weyr had encountered in Bown or in the Fields of Westum. A bird called. Weyr could not identify the bird. Weyr heard a regular distant pulsating roar. It reminded him of rushing water, but the sound was much more powerful than that of water in a river or a stream.

The pictures and the sounds and smells were not unpleasant, but in a corner of his awareness, Weyr found them unsettling. There was a dim pain to the sensations. Weyr felt as though he wanted something but could not exactly tell what it was.

Weyr did not know how long the visions and sounds and smells lasted. That was not unusual. During meditation, time lost its meaning. Gradually Weyr came back into his normal consciousness. He was relaxed as he always was after he had meditated. But he had full memory of what had happened to him during meditation. Usually the sensations of meditation, vivid when they came, were fleeting, seldom remembered afterward.

These had come from the south. Fully conscious now, Weyr was sure of that. Although he was again aware of his surroundings, of the growing heat, of the pond and the Agari camp below, Weyr could still sense the green grove. He felt as though he could almost reach out and pick one of the oval yellow fruits, taste its moist, slightly tart flavor. . . .

Abruptly the memories vanished, and Weyr became aware of another sensation.

Someone, Weyr knew, was watching him.

~

Weyr stood up and looked around the clearing. He could see no one, but he was certain he was being watched. He focused on a cluster of low shrubs about twenty feet to his left. There. Perhaps his senses had extended again for an instant. Or perhaps he had only noticed a slight movement in the leaves. Either way, he was certain that whoever was watching him stood behind the shrubs.

"Who's there?" Weyr said. "I can see you. Who's there?"

The shrubs parted. A boy about Weyr's size stepped lightly into the clearing. His skin was fair, his nose narrow and pointed, his shoulder-length hair blond. He wore brightly colored blue-and-orange trousers and an open-necked red-and-yellow shirt. A frown creased his forehead.

"Who are you?" Weyr said. "What do you want?"

"Who are *you*?" the other boy said. "And what do *you* want?"

The boy spoke in Tam, but with a slight accent. His voice sounded arrogant. Weyr felt the muscles on the back of his neck tighten.

"What are you doing here?" the boy asked.

"I was just med . . ." Weyr began, and stopped. He did not need to explain himself. "I was minding my own affairs," Weyr concluded, "which are none of yours."

"It's my affair if you were spying on us," the other boy said.

"Spying on who?" Weyr said. "Who are you, anyway?"

"I am Kamlar, son of Lakren, the Instrument of the Merchants of Elubin," the boy said. He sounded proud. He jerked his head toward the pond. "That's our party down there. If you're spying on us, that's my affair. And my father's. Who are you?"

"My name is Weyr."

"Weyr the Tam."

"Yes, I'm Tam. You're Agari."

"What else? Well, Weyr the Tam, you'll have to come with me to see my father."

Weyr shifted his feet to place one behind the other, arched his shoulders, and bent his knees slightly in the hint of a crouch. The relaxation that had come after meditation was gone. He was completely alert, his muscles tense.

"And why should I do that?" Weyr said.

"Because I say so."

"Ab splatter!" Weyr said. "That's no reason. I have a right to be here. Just as much right as you do. I was minding my own affairs. That's more than I can say about you."

"You'd better come with me!" Kamlar said.

"You can't make me do anything," Weyr said.

The Agari boy crouched slightly and thrust his head forward.

"We'll see about that," Kamlar said.

Kamlar dropped into a full crouch, his arms tensed away from his body. He moved slowly to his right, circling Weyr. The other boy was no bigger than he was, Weyr thought, though he looked strong and well muscled. Weyr knew that he himself was strong for his size. It would be an equal fight. Weyr crouched, too, his weight forward on the balls of his feet. He followed Kamlar as the Agari boy circled him.

Kamlar stopped for a moment, made a feinting movement to his left, and rushed at Weyr.

Chapter Five

W EYR FELT KAMLAR'S hands lock onto his neck just above the shoulders. He flung his arms up inside the boy's hold and gripped him in the same way. For a moment they clung together like that, circling, struggling for advantage. Kamlar pulled one arm free from Weyr's neck. Weyr grabbed at the arm and missed. A hard fist struck Weyr's stomach. The breath hissed out of him. His vision blurred for an instant. Weyr felt his grip on Kamlar's neck loosen.

With his free arm Weyr swung in a wide arc toward Kamlar's face. His fist crunched against bone. Kamlar grunted and lurched away. Blood oozed from his nose and one corner of his mouth. Kamlar wiped at it with his arm. A red stain spread on his yellow sleeve. Weyr got his breath back. His vision cleared. He moved toward Kamlar again.

Weyr got in two quick swipes at Kamlar's face. He took another fist at his own midsection, a glancing blow slightly off center this time but still enough to make him gasp again. Kamlar retreated a step. He caught Weyr's right eye with a solid jab as he moved back. Weyr landed a wild swing on Kamlar's cheek and another on the other boy's chest. They circled each other again, sparring with light punches.

Kamlar closed in on Weyr once more. He grabbed Weyr around the waist with one hand. With his other hand he pushed hard at Weyr's chin. His fingers ground into Weyr's cheek just below the eye.

Weyr held his footing. He felt Kamlar's leg slip slightly. Weyr snaked his own leg behind Kamlar's knee and pushed hard against his chest with both hands. Kamlar fell heavily on his back and rolled slightly to one side. Weyr leaped onto him. With one motion, he turned Kamlar onto his stomach, sat on his back, and twisted his right arm up below his shoulder blade.

"Don't move or I'll break your arm," Weyr said. He tasted salt. He was bleeding inside his mouth.

Kamlar squirmed. Weyr pushed the boy's arm farther up into the small of his back.

"I mean it!" Weyr said. "I've got you."

"I slipped on something," Kamlar said between his teeth.

"Doesn't matter. I've still got you," Weyr said. He spat blood, then took a deep breath. "Now, Kamlar the Agari, tell me I have a right to be here, as much right as you have."

Kamlar was silent. Weyr twisted the boy's wrist. Kamlar grunted.

"Tell me!"

Kamlar still said nothing. Weyr put more pressure on his arm. He pushed Kamlar's face into the ground.

"You have a right to be here," Kamlar said into the dirt.

"Tell me it's not your affair why I'm here," Weyr said.

"It's . . . not . . . my affair," Kamlar said. "Now let me go."

"Only if you agree to leave me alone," Weyr said. His eye hurt. It was beginning to swell, he realized. "Promise to leave me alone."

"I promise."

"Make it an oath," Weyr said. "Say an oath on whatever you Agari swear oaths on."

Kamlar hesitated. Weyr pulled back a finger on Kamlar's imprisoned hand. Kamlar yelped.

"All right," Kamlar said. "I swear it on the Tomb of Aluan."

It was not an oath Weyr knew, but it sounded serious enough. Weyr let go of Kamlar's finger.

"Now let me up," Kamlar said.

Weyr released Kamlar's arm, swung off his back, and settled heavily onto the ground. He put a hand to his eye and touched it gently. It felt puffy. His lip felt tender and puffy when he touched it, too. There was blood on his finger when he took it away from his lip.

Kamlar rolled over onto his back and struggled up to a sitting position. He ran his hand up and down the arm Weyr had twisted. The blood on his sleeve had turned dark. Dirt mixed with dried blood caked his chin. Kamlar wiped at it with his sleeve. He looked at Weyr, an astonished expression on his face.

"You can fight," Kamlar said. "I slipped or you wouldn't have gotten me, but you still sure can fight. Tam aren't supposed to be very good at fighting nowadays, except for the border guards and maybe the street brats in Domn.

People say they're all half Agari, anyway. But you're a Tam and you can fight."

"I'm not a street brat," Weyr said. He wondered for an instant what street brats were. "But I can fight if I have to."

"I guess so!" Kamlar said. He hesitated, still rubbing his arm. "Now will you tell me what you're doing here?"

Weyr half rose. Kamlar held out his hands to ward him off.

"I'm not ordering you to tell me," Kamlar said. "I took an oath, remember? I'm only asking. Only if you want to tell me."

"I wasn't spying," Weyr said. "Why would anyone want to spy on you?"

"There are people around here who don't like the Agari. Lots of Tam don't like Agari," Kamlar said. "That's why my father has guards. We have to be careful. If you weren't spying, what were you doing?"

"I was meditating," Weyr said.

"Meditating," Kamlar said. He frowned for a moment, as though trying to remember something. "I've heard my father talk about that. What is it?"

"It's hard to explain," Weyr said. "You just relax and let your thoughts go the way they want to. It clears the mind."

"Maybe I should try it, if it makes you able to fight like that," Kamlar said. "How old are you?"

"About thirteen," Weyr said.

"*About* thirteen? Don't you know?" Kamlar's tone was both astonished and arrogant.

"My parents died in a flood when I was little," Weyr

said. "Nobody else knew exactly how old I was. How old are you?"

"Thirteen. I'll be fourteen next Month of the Bear. Do you live around here?"

"No. I come from up north. I'm just traveling through. My cousin lives in Domn. I'm going there to live with him."

"Where's your family?"

"I don't have any family. My gran died and I didn't have any other family. She told me to go to my cousin if something happened to her."

"You're on your own?" Kamlar said, a note of wonder in his voice. There was no arrogance to his tone now.

"I have been."

"For how long?"

"A little more than a nineday."

Kamlar gave a low whistle. "It must be something to be on your own, without any family," he said. "My family hardly lets me out of their sight, whether it's my father or Romely."

"Who's Romely?"

"My cousin. She took care of me after my mother died. She's in Keytho now, I think. You've really been all by yourself?"

"I was. Now I'm going to Domn with Nomer and Relinda. They're part of your party, aren't they?"

"Ab splatter!" Kamlar said. "Nomer and Relinda are under my father's protection. He brought them with him from Carda. Why didn't you say you were with them?"

"What I was doing was none of your affair," Weyr said. "You admitted that."

"You forced me."

"That doesn't matter. You admitted it."

"All right. It still would have been better if you'd said you were with Nomer and Relinda. I wouldn't have had to fight you then. I shouldn't have fought you. If you're with Nomer and Relinda, you're under my father's protection. For that matter, you're supposed to be under my protection, too."

Weyr snorted in irritation. He had merely agreed to travel with Nomer and Relinda. He had not agreed to be protected by anyone.

"I don't need your protection. Or your father's," Weyr said stiffly. "I get along well enough by myself."

"I believe that," Kamlar said. His face took on an anxious expression. "Still, if you're with Nomer and Relinda, my father is obliged to do for you what he does for them. That's the Agari Way." Kamlar struck his palm with his fist. "By The Comet! Here it is, the first time my father has ever let me come with him when he travels. And now I've fought with someone he's supposed to protect. He'll be mad as an ab bull in rut when he finds out I gave you that."

Kamlar pointed at Weyr's eye. His fingers were short and blunt. Weyr touched the flesh under his eye. He could imagine what it looked like. Weyr wondered what had he gotten himself into. "The Instrument has seen fit to take us under his protection," Nomer had said. "Which is not necessarily a bad thing." Now, Weyr thought, the "us" apparently included him.

"Your father's an important man, isn't he?" Weyr said.

"In Domn, yes," Kamlar said.

"If Nomer and Relinda find out that I gave you that

bloody nose and they're part of your father's party, they won't be too happy either, I guess," Weyr said.

"I hadn't thought of that."

Weyr grinned. Grinning made his lip hurt.

"Maybe Nomer and Relinda and your father don't need to find out what happened," Weyr said.

"That's ridiculous," Kamlar said. He looked at the bloodstains on his sleeve, then fingered his bruised nose and cut lip. "How could they not find out? We look a mess, both of us."

"You slipped, remember?" Weyr said. "There are a lot of trees and bare roots and rocks and things up here. You must have slipped on one of them and hit yourself when you fell."

"And you?"

"I must have slipped and hit myself, too," Weyr said.

Kamlar stared at Weyr. His eyes were the color of the sky on a clear summer day. A grin cracked his face. The cut on his lip and the caked blood on his chin made the grin look more like a grimace.

"Some slips," Kamlar said.

"I guess so," Weyr said. He grinned again. His lip hurt less than it had before.

Kamlar threw back his head and laughed. "Slips like nobody ever had before," he said.

"Nobody. Ever," Weyr said. He laughed, too.

~

"Sweet, sweet Breath of Life, Weyr!" Nomer said. "What happened to you? You look like you've been rooting around in a stable. And where in Seven Levels of Torment have you been? We've been waiting. Are you all right?"

Nomer sat at the front of the multicolored wagon, the reins of the single horse held lightly in his huge hands. Relinda and Berthin sat beside him. Relinda had Weyr's pack on her lap. Ahead of Nomer and Relinda's wagon, the Agari guards were mounted on horseback in a haphazard line with the Agari wagons between them. Kamlar was somewhere near the front of the line. He and Weyr had separated as they approached the Agari party.

"I'm fine," Weyr said. "I just had an accident. I met Kamlar in the woods and . . ."

"Kamlar? The Instrument's son?" Nomer said. He sounded alarmed. "What did you do? Did anything happen to Kamlar? We're . . ."

". . . under the Instrument's protection," Weyr said.

"Yes. What did you and Kamlar do?"

"We . . . met . . . in the woods," Weyr said. "We had an accident. We both slipped and fell and . . ."

"Nomer!" said a commanding tenor voice.

Weyr turned. An Agari man who sat a roan horse with an elaborately decorated saddle rode toward him. Weyr did not need to be told that the man was the Agari Instrument, Kamlar's father. The family resemblance was striking. The Instrument had the same pointed nose and blue eyes as Kamlar and hair only a shade darker. But he had a small, trim beard. Weyr realized with a start that the beard had been dyed purple. Some Tamish women travelers who came through Bown had worn their hair dyed, but Weyr had never seen a man with colored hair before.

The Agari Instrument was not a large man, but he looked impressive as he wheeled his horse up beside Nomer and Relinda's wagon. His body was compact and muscular, and he sat the animal, Weyr thought, like someone who was used to being obeyed. The Instrument was, Weyr guessed, about Nomer's age. Kamlar walked beside his father's horse. His face was still grimed with dirt and dried blood, as it had been when Weyr had left him. He nodded shyly at Weyr.

"Yes, Instrument?" Nomer said in Tam. Weyr heard respect in Nomer's voice, but not fear.

"Is this child with you?" the Instrument said, also in Tam. He pointed at Weyr. A ring with a large, blue gem sparkled on his finger.

"He is," Nomer said. "He joined us last night."

"He looks like a street brat," the Instrument said. "As does my son. Have you discovered what occurred?"

"The boy claims he had an accident in the woods when he was with Kamlar," Nomer said.

"And you believe him?"

"I wasn't there, Instrument," Nomer said. He shrugged his huge shoulders. "He went into the woods to meditate."

"It is not my impression that the Tamish custom of meditation ordinarily leaves one with a swollen eye and a cut lip," the Instrument said. "Not to mention assorted other bruises and a thick layer of dirt."

"No, Instrument, nor is it mine," Nomer said. "Still, the boy claims he met with an accident, slipped and fell . . ."

"My son tells a similar story," the Instrument said. "Kamlar, I ask you again. Is that what took place?"

Kamlar bit his lip. He did not look at his father.

"Yes, Father," Kamlar said.

"You, boy," the Instrument said to Weyr. "What's your name?"

"Weyr, si'be," Weyr said. He bowed from the waist.

"You are, of course, Tam."

"Yes, si'be."

"You have the same story to tell? You and my son happened to meet in the woods, and you both slipped and fell?"

Weyr glanced at Kamlar. The Agari boy bit his lip again and fidgeted uneasily. But there was a glint in his eye.

"Yes, si'be," Weyr said. He swallowed hard. "That's the way it was."

The Instrument glared at Weyr. His eyes were as blue as Kamlar's. Weyr wanted to avert his own eyes, but he tried to look back steadily at the impressive man on the roan horse. After a moment the Instrument turned to glare at Kamlar. Kamlar lifted his head and looked directly at his father, his chin tilted slightly upward.

The Instrument began to laugh. His laughter reminded Weyr of the sound of a night owl. The oddly colored purple beard waggled with each hoot. The laugh subsided to a chuckle.

"I must warn my guards about the woods," the Instrument said. "It would appear that there are dangers there that we do not know about. I certainly would not want one of the guards to slip and fall."

The Instrument hooted with laughter another time. He looked first at Kamlar, then at Weyr.

"Or perhaps," the Instrument said, "the dangers in the woods apply only to boys. I do seem to recall encountering dangers not unlike the one that appears to have befallen these two when I was much the same age. Is that not so, Nomer?"

"I have similar memories, Instrument," Nomer said.

"An unfortunate accident, then, and best forgotten," the Instrument said. Again he looked at Kamlar and then at Weyr. His narrow nose wrinkled in disgust. "Nevertheless, it would be good if the victims of this unfortunate accident were to avail themselves of the pond to clean themselves before we move on. We have already waited for them. A few more minutes cannot be too important. It does not seem a good idea for the son of the Instrument of the Merchants of Elubin and a . . . a companion with whom he has met an unfortunate accident . . . to travel looking like street brats."

Weyr looked at Nomer. The barest hint of a smile cracked one corner of Nomer's lips.

"You'd better do what the Instrument says, Weyr," Nomer said.

"All right," Weyr said.

Weyr started down toward the pond. Kamlar fell in step beside him.

"Oh, Weyr," Nomer said behind him.

"Yes?" Weyr said. He turned back toward Nomer.

"Try not to get into any more accidents when you're meditating," Nomer said. "It's enough to scare me off the whole custom, and I've come to rather like it."

"I'll try, Nomer," Weyr said.

~

Weyr's lip and eye still throbbed as he walked up from the pond with Kamlar toward the Agari party. Following Kamlar's lead, he had stripped to the waist and washed off most of the grime that caked his face and arms. His clothes were still dusty.

The Instrument waited near the head of the line of horses and wagons. A single riderless horse stood behind him. The horse was smaller than the Instrument's roan, and it was dun colored, but it looked strong and well kept. Kamlar walked to it, put his foot in a stirrup, and vaulted easily into the saddle. Weyr hesitated a moment, then turned to go back toward Nomer and Relinda's wagon at the rear of the Agari party.

"You can ride with me, if you want to, Weyr," Kamlar said.

Kamlar lifted his foot out of the stirrup nearest Weyr. Weyr hesitated. He had seldom ridden horses, and certainly he had never ridden so fine a one as this.

"Have you ridden much?" Kamlar said.

"Not very much," Weyr said.

"Here, I'll give you a hand up."

Weyr grasped Kamlar's hand and put a foot in the empty stirrup. With the other boy's help, he managed to set himself on the horse behind Kamlar.

"Thanks, Kamlar," Weyr said.

"You should call me Kam," the other boy said. "That's what people in my family call me."

"Kam," Weyr said.

"If you haven't done a lot of riding, you'd better hold on tight," Kamlar said. "You don't want to slip and have another accident."

"You'd better hold on tight, too, Kam," Weyr said. "One accident is enough for one day."

Kamlar laughed.

"Enough for both of us," Kamlar said.

Chapter Six

THE AGARI, Weyr thought, had to be the noisiest people he had ever met. The Instrument's party went two or three abreast along The Great Way. With the wagons and the guards, they made a substantial caravan. As the party traveled the dusty road, they created a cacophony of sound. The guards yelled to one another, the Instrument shouted at the guards or at Kamlar, Kamlar yelled to his father, Nomer boomed out comments to the others. It seemed to Weyr that only he and Relinda — the two Tam in the party — did not regularly shout.

Weyr could not understand anything the Agari men cried out to one another. At first he thought they were arguing. But Kamlar assured him that there was no argument.

"We just shout," Kamlar said. "That's the Agari Way."

The Agari also sang loudly. Weyr found that easier to get used to. Nomer and Relinda usually began the songs from their wagon at the rear of the party. Nomer's deep, resonant bass sounded out the first few words. Then Relinda joined in. Her singing voice was a powerful, richly textured low soprano. Both voices carried easily the full length of the caravan. Most of the songs they began were rollicking and rhythmic, like the one Nomer had sung that morning. They had repetitive choruses, in which the guards joined enthusiastically and noisily.

The music sounded strange to Weyr. The rhythms seemed more complex than those of the Tamish songs he had sung in Bown, and many of the melodies had an odd, almost plaintive, quality to them. Weyr had always liked to sing. He found it fairly easy to pick up the melodies, and, by repetition, some of the Agari words. Occasionally he even improvised a few notes of harmony.

"You've got a good, strong voice, Weyr," Kamlar said as they dismounted to eat their midday meal after a series of songs. "I envy you that."

"Your voice is all right," Weyr said.

"There's no need to be polite," Kamlar said. "I can't sing. I'm like my father that way. He loves music, and so do I, but when he sings he sounds like a drunken ab."

Weyr raised his eyebrows.

"Maybe I shouldn't say that about my father," Kamlar said. "But I'm only quoting him. He says it about himself."

Kamlar was no more than honest, Weyr thought, when he listened more carefully to the Instrument's voice. The Agari man sang, if that was the right word, in a dull monotone. Kamlar's voice was not much better.

As the day went on, Weyr became a little more accustomed to the din of Agari voices, Kamlar's and the Instrument's among them. But he was glad when evening came and he headed back for the relative quiet of Nomer and Relinda's wagon at the edge of the Agari camp.

Weyr gathered wood for the cooking fire at which Relinda had begun to work, then undid his bedroll and sat
down on it. He could still feel some of the bruises from
his fight with Kamlar. Idly, Weyr watched Nomer as he
entertained Berthin by apparently pulling scarfs out of
nowhere. Nomer was obviously a skilled magician. Weyr
could not imagine how he made the scarfs appear.

Finally Nomer went off in the direction of the Instrument's tent. Weyr half dozed for a few minutes until Berthin joined him.

"Did you see Nomer's tricks?" Berthin said.

"Yes," Weyr said. "He's good. Do you know how he
does them?"

"No," Berthin said. Her pale-blue eyes glinted mischie-
vously. "But Nomer's a witch, you know."

"Berth!" Relinda said.

Weyr threw up his hands in mock alarm. "By The
Comet!" he said to Berthin. "Is Nomer, now? And just
what kind of a witch is he?"

"Oh, a good witch," Berthin said.

"Well, I should hope so," Weyr said. "Tell me, though.
Does he use his witchcraft with you when you're
naughty?"

Berthin pondered the question for a moment.

"I'm never naughty," Berthin said.

"No?"

"No." Berthin eyed Weyr. She flicked her head so one
of her braids flopped over her right shoulder. "But sometimes I like to tease."

"Like father, like daughter," Relinda said drily.

"I guess sometimes I like to tease, too," Weyr said.

Berthin giggled. "Good," she said. "Then we can tease each other all the way to Domn."

"Now I've got three of them," Relinda said. She rolled her eyes up.

Weyr laughed. Relinda straightened up from the cooking fire.

"This will do all right on its own for a while," Relinda said. "Let's be on our way, Berth."

"Relinda and I are going down to the water to take a bath," Berthin said.

The Agari party had camped along the banks of a meandering small river. Berthin pointed toward a clump of low green bushes beside the water a short distance upstream.

Weyr wiped a hand through his hair. His fingers came out gritty with dust. He stood up. "That's a fine idea," he said. "I'll come with you."

"No, no, no, Weyr!" Berthin said. "You can't come with us. Boys don't take baths with girls."

"They don't?" Weyr said, startled. Boys and girls, and, for that matter, men and women, had always bathed together in the River Bardon near Bown.

"It's just not done," Berthin said firmly. "Isn't that so, Relinda?"

"That's so among the Agari," Relinda said.

Weyr felt blood rush to his cheeks. "I'm sorry," he said. "I didn't know. Back in Bown, we . . ."

"Don't be embarrassed, Weyr," Relinda said. "In the little village where I was born, nobody made a fuss about men and women bathing together. But the Agari have their own ways about such things. I had to learn."

"You haven't always lived with the Agari?"

"Oh, my, no," Relinda said. "I saw a few Agari as I grew up — they're more common near Domn than here — but Nomer was the first one I ever really got to know. That was after I left my village. And it was only much later that I met a great many Agari."

"When you first met them, did you think the Agari were a little . . . *unusual*?" Weyr said cautiously. "I don't mean Nomer," he added quickly. "But the others."

"Even Nomer, sometimes," Relinda said with a wry smile. "What with their boisterousness and their funny earnestness — and the ridiculous way they protect their women — I thought they were all quite strange."

"What did you do?"

Loud male voices rang from a spot near the stream behind Weyr.

"Do you know the Tamish proverb about the sheep?" Relinda said.

"You mean, 'If you're going to keep company with sheep, it's good to learn how to say 'baah'?" Weyr said.

"Just so. Sometimes, I found, that was the best thing to do," Relinda said. She pointed in the direction from which the male voices had sounded. "You'd better go bathe with the men."

"All right," Weyr said. He started to walk in the direction Relinda had pointed.

"Weyr?" Berthin said.

Weyr turned around. Berthin put her hands on either

side of her head as though they were ears. She wiggled her fingers.

"B-a-a-a-a-h!" Berthin said.

Weyr smiled ruefully. "B-a-a-a-a-h, yourself," he said.

~

In a small pool formed by a bend in the river, the Instrument and most of his guards, all naked, laughed and shouted to one another. As Weyr began to undress, he heard a loud bass voice bellow. He looked up. Nomer ran along the opposite bank of the river, leaped off, doubled up his legs under him, and landed with a huge splash near the Instrument. The Instrument uttered his peculiar hooting laugh and slapped his hands on the water, bringing a small geyser up into Nomer's face. Nomer responded in kind. A ruddy-cheeked guard ducked under the pool and came up pushing handfuls of water at both Nomer and the Instrument. A second guard did the same thing. Within moments, everyone in the pool, including the Instrument, was engaged in a full-fledged water fight.

Weyr's jaw dropped. What were grown men doing conducting themselves so? Tamish adults would never do such a thing. And the Instrument! No Tam who held an impressive title would behave that way. Did the Agari have no sense of dignity?

His eye still on the water fight, Weyr bent to slip the last of his clothing off his legs. A gush of water caught him full in the face. Weyr saw Kamlar in the pool just below him.

"Come on in, Weyr," Kamlar shouted.

Weyr hesitated for a moment. Another gush of water

caught him. This time it was Nomer, who had come up near Kamlar.

Weyr threw up his hands. Clearly there was only one thing to do.

"B-a-a-a-a-h!" Weyr bleated. He leaped into the air, his legs curled under him, and landed in the pool near Nomer and Kamlar.

When Weyr came up, Nomer, Kamlar, and one of the guards all pummeled him with water. Weyr fought back, and soon he was in the thick of the fight. He laughed and yelled, yelled and splashed, splashed and got dowsed. A few times he even sent a spray of water toward the Instrument. The Agari man did not seem to mind.

Finally the furor subsided. Laughing and panting, Weyr leaned against an overhanging branch to catch his breath. Nomer waded up beside him and put his right arm on the branch near Weyr. There was an oddly shaped small blue scar on Nomer's shoulder. Nomer rubbed at it absently.

"Now I guess you can consider yourself officially welcomed among the Instrument's party," Nomer said. He chuckled.

"Is it always like that when Agaris take baths?" Weyr said.

"Often enough," Nomer said. "For the males at least. I guess the women are more sedate. Relinda calls us 'men who never quite got over being boys.' But I like it."

"I like it too," Weyr said.

"I thought you might," Nomer said.

Nomer moved away to talk with the Instrument. Kamlar, still a little out of breath, came up and leaned against the branch.

"What a fight!" Kamlar said. "I even got my father a couple of times. That was fun, wasn't it?"

"Yes," Weyr said.

Weyr blinked. Kamlar had a scar on his right shoulder the same shape as the one Nomer had. Kamlar's scar was green, and it appeared to be newer than Nomer's, but otherwise it was virtually identical. The scar, Weyr saw, looked like a small sword with a curved blade and curved ends on the handle. Weyr glanced around him. Every one of the guards had the same scar. Some were red, some green, some blue. The Instrument had a purple scar on his arm. Perhaps the scars were birthmarks. But were all Agari born with an identical birthmark? Weyr supposed that was possible, but it certainly seemed strange.

"Weyr, what's wrong?" Kamlar said.

Weyr realized he had been frowning in puzzlement. "Nothing's wrong," Weyr said. "But, well, say so if it's none of my affair, but do all Agari have that birthmark on their shoulders?"

"It's not a birthmark," Kamlar said. "It's called an adolo. And only Agari men have it."

"What is it?"

"Back in ancient times when all Agari men were supposed to be warriors, you got it when you killed your first man in battle," Kamlar said. "Now boys just get it when they're about my age. I got mine a few months ago."

"It grows on your shoulder when you get to be that old?" Weyr said.

Kamlar laughed. "No, no. They put it on you. There's a ceremony that goes with it. They cut you with a special knife and then put colored dye under your skin."

Weyr winced. "Doesn't that hurt?" he said.

"It hurts some, for a while," Kamlar said.

"But you still let them do it to you?"

"It's not a matter of *let*," Kamlar said. "I *wanted* them to do it. Getting your adolo is supposed to mean you're officially grown up." Kamlar smiled wistfully. "Sometimes I wish my father really believed that. But at least Father let me come on this trip with him. He never would have done that if I hadn't reached adolo age."

Weyr shook his head. "I never heard of anything like that," he said.

"It's the Agari Way," Kamlar said.

~

That seemed to be Kamlar's explanation for everything when Weyr asked him more questions as the days passed. Things were always just done "the Agari Way."

The guards, for example, were part of the "Way." Kamlar took it as a matter of course that the guards were all men.

"Agari women simply do not fight," Kamlar said when Weyr asked him about the matter.

Kamlar also took it as a matter of course that the guards would follow members of the Instrument's party wherever they went. When Weyr and Kamlar ventured into one of the little villages along The Great Way, they were always accompanied by one or two of the armed men. Weyr felt uncomfortable with the guards' presence, particularly because, except for one ruddy-cheeked man named Valmo who spoke a little Tam, he could not communicate with them at all. But it was clear that when Kamlar had said that Weyr, as Nomer and Relinda's guest, was also "under the Instrument's protection," he had spoken only the simple truth.

The Instrument himself was another puzzling part of the "Way." Weyr could not understand the manner in which he treated his guards. Sometimes he was jovial with them, laughing and joking as they went along the road. But sometimes he barked out orders to them in rapid Agari. The men always jumped to obey. Once Weyr saw him scold a guard in such harsh tones that the man was almost in tears. It was hard to figure out how the guards knew what to expect from the Instrument.

Weyr was not sure what *he* should expect from him, either. When the Instrument spoke to Weyr, he was always respectful and even, in a brusque way, kind. But for the most part, to Weyr's relief, the man ignored him. So Weyr was surprised — and, he admitted to himself, a little wary — when the Instrument finally said something directly to Kamlar about him.

"Kam, you should introduce your companion to shan," the Instrument said as Weyr and Kamlar dismounted at the end of one day.

"Who is Shan?" Weyr asked Kamlar when the Instrument had left.

"Not *who*. *What*," Kamlar said. "Shan is a game. Most Agaris play shan."

"It's part of the Agari Way?" Weyr said.

Kamlar laughed. "You could say that. At least my father sets great store by it. I'm not a very good player, but I can teach you. Want to learn?" Weyr nodded. "After dinner, come on over."

When Weyr later made his way to the Agari camp, he found Kamlar seated cross-legged on the ground outside a green and orange tent. In front of him was a small square board crisscrossed with straight lines to make smaller squares.

"This is shan," Kamlar said. "The idea of it is easy to understand. It's the playing that's hard."

Kamlar pointed to four areas on the board, each made up of nine small squares. The areas were marked off as what Kamlar called Spirit of the Home spaces, or, more usually, simply Home spaces. The object of the game was to capture your opponent's Home spaces while protecting your own. As many as four people could play.

To play, one placed small round pieces on the intersections of the lines or moved them from one intersection to another. The pieces for Kamlar's game were made of beautifully carved stone with a different color for each player, but, Kamlar told Weyr, people often made them out of wood. Players started out with a fixed number of pieces. The rules for moving or adding them on the board were relatively simple, but as more and more pieces were placed, the relationships among them became extremely complicated. One had to be aware of many parts of the board at once. An advantage in one area might leave one vulnerable elsewhere.

The game seemed strange to Weyr. Everything depended on the placement of the pieces. There was no element of chance in it. Weyr had never played a game that did not include some chance. At first the complicated relationships among the pieces bewildered Weyr. Kamlar beat him quickly in two games. But then Weyr began to catch on a little. The third game lasted much longer before Weyr finally lost.

Off and on during the next day, Weyr found himself visualizing the shan board in his head. Mentally he placed pieces in one position or another, imagining what Kamlar's countermove might be. For some reason, the intricate symmetry and precise regularity of the patterns on the board intrigued him. That night he managed to hold his own for the entire evening before Kamlar finally eked out a victory.

Weyr thought about shan a good deal as the two boys began to play nearly every evening. Often the Instrument and Nomer set up another board near them and played shan themselves, though they never invited the boys to join them in a four-person game. Both men seemed to concentrate intensely as they played, but occasionally they called Kamlar and Weyr over to observe a particularly interesting situation on the board. And a few times the Instrument watched Kamlar and Weyr's game and made suggestions to Weyr about strategy.

"You seem to have a remarkably good sense of the game for a neophyte," the Instrument told Weyr on one such occasion. "Almost an Agari sense of it. Keep at it, my boy, keep at it."

Weyr knew the Instrument had intended to compliment him, but was not sure he liked the idea that he had an "Agari sense" of anything. It was one thing, he thought, to learn to say "baah" when you were in the company of sheep. It was another to become a sheep yourself. Still, it was obviously better to have the Instrument pleased with him than not. And he was certain about one thing. Shan was one part of the Agari Way he liked a lot.

~

If Weyr was learning about the Agari Way from Kamlar, the other boy was obviously also very interested in what Weyr knew and what Weyr had done before he had joined the Agari party. The fact that Weyr had been traveling alone, without any family, seemed almost incredible to Kamlar. Kamlar plied Weyr with questions about where he had gone, what had happened to him, and how he had managed on his own, until Weyr began to wonder whether Kamlar ever did anything by himself away from his family or without his father's presence or permission.

Kamlar seemed curious, too, about what Weyr began to think of, despite himself, as the Tamish Way. At Kamlar's request, Weyr taught him how to meditate. Most mornings before breakfast they met and found a quiet spot for meditation. When they went together into a village, Kamlar was always full of questions about what they heard and saw. While Kamlar seemed to know some things about the Tam, he was woefully ignorant about other things. At one point Weyr mentioned that he had made money betting salam just before he had joined the Agari party.

"Do you do that a lot?" Kamlar asked. "Bet on the salam races?"

"I bet some," Weyr said. "Not as much as most. People back in Bown thought I was a little odd because I didn't bet as often as other people. Don't you bet salam?"

"No. I've seen Tam doing it in Domn. On the streets mostly. I never got too close. And I've certainly never bet."

Weyr blinked in surprise. He had never met anyone above the age of six or seven who did not bet salam. Tam children even younger wagered for colored rocks or other trinkets on made-up races.

"Agari don't race salam?"

"Not many of them."

"Don't Agari gamble?" Weyr said.

"Of course they do. I know Nomer does. My father says he's a little Tamish at heart that way," Kamlar said. "Even my father bets sometimes at the gambling places in Domn. But my . . . my father doesn't like it too much if I gamble."

There was something wistful in Kamlar's voice, Weyr thought. On impulse, Weyr said, "Would you like to see a salam race? It shouldn't be too hard to find one. I guess you wouldn't have to bet. You could just watch."

Kamlar was silent for a moment.

"I suppose my father wouldn't mind if I only watched," Kamlar said. "Maybe he'd think it was part of my 'Tamish education.'"

"Your what?"

"My 'Tamish education,'" Kamlar said in a slightly sarcastic tone. "That's why my father let me come along with him on this trip, you know. I'm supposed to be finding out about the Tam — the ones outside Domn, that is. 'Broadening my knowledge' of them, my father says."

"You mean you're supposed to spy on the Tam?" Weyr said. "Like you thought I was spying on your father's party?"

Kamlar's pale cheeks flushed.

"That was a ridiculous idea," Kamlar said. "I wouldn't have said that if I'd thought about it. I guess I was, well, just kind of bored. Nothing much had happened on the trip up until then. My father went to his meetings and I stayed with the guards. So when I finally slipped away from the guards for a little while and then ran into you, I sort of . . . made up . . . that business about spying." Kamlar shrugged. "Not that there aren't Tam who hate the Agari. But they'd hardly use someone our age as a spy."

"Still, your father wants you to spy on the Tam?"

"Not spy, exactly," Kamlar said. "I'm supposed to *learn* about the Tam. So I'll understand them better. When I grow up, I'll probably do the same work my father does. That's the Agari Way. My father represents the Agari merchants in a Tamish area. So he has to know about the Tam. And I'm supposed to know, too."

"Is that why you've been asking me so many questions?" Weyr said.

"Maybe a little," Kamlar said. His face flushed again. He looked at the ground. "Not really though. That's just my father's idea. It's not mine. I . . . well . . . I just kind of enjoy being with you. I've never met anybody like you. I told you it was a pretty dull trip until you came along." Kamlar looked back at Weyr, his chin tilted upward. "Besides, you ask me just as many questions about the Agari as I ask you about the Tam."

That was true enough, Weyr thought.

"It was a pretty dull trip for me until I met you, too," Weyr said. "Maybe we're spying on each other."

Kamlar laughed. "Maybe so," he said.

"Well, I guess you can't understand much about Tam if you don't spy on at least one salam race," Weyr said.

Chapter Seven

T HE NEXT EVENING Weyr and Kamlar, followed by
Valmo, the guard who spoke some Tam, made their
way into a village near the Agari camp. Weyr did not
have to ask after a salam race. As soon as they neared
the village's small market area, he heard the familiar
sounds.

"Half a copper on the yellow-green with the shoulder
scar to dominate," a voice shouted.

"Covered," another voice cried.

"A copper at double on the bright green for the crat
kill," someone else said. "Who'll cover double on crat kill
for the bright green?"

Weyr smiled broadly and quickened his pace. He had
not seen a salam race since he had joined the Agari party.

The racing crowd did not look too large — there were
perhaps fifty people — but it was enthusiastic and noisy.
Weyr led Kamlar through the crowd to the front — there
were advantages to being small — while Valmo, with
some effort, pushed in to stand behind them. A few people

glanced at Valmo and Kamlar, but most, if they noticed the Agari at all, were either too polite or too engrossed in the race to make a point of it.

Weyr's eyebrows shot up when he saw the salam field. It was much more elaborate than the one in Bown, though Weyr had seen permanent salam fields like it at the Grand Market. The shape was normal — it was an octagon perhaps ten feet across — but the knee-high adobe walls were festooned with pastel-colored triangular banners on poles at each corner, and the walls had been dyed a dull red. The small reed crat cage in the center of the field had a banner attached to it as well. Weyr heard the unique shrill whistle of the insect as it scurried frantically around inside the cage, trying in vain to escape from the salam on the packed earth around it. He felt in his pocket to make sure he had coins for betting.

The race had a full complement of eight salam. The owners of the lizards racing this round knelt or crouched beside the banners at the corners of the field, urging their racers on. Several salam crawled around the field in seemingly aimless motion.

A dull-green lizard perhaps six inches long with a stump of a tail lay motionless a few inches from the crat cage, facing the insect inside. Weyr eyed it keenly. He shook his head. The lizard looked listless. Still, you could never tell with salam. Perhaps, as a long shot, he should offer odds on. . . .

"How do you bet?" Kamlar said.

"What?" Weyr said. He had momentarily forgotten Kamlar was with him. "Oh. The simplest bet is on the crat kill. Which lizard gets the bug in the cage."

"Is that green one that's closest to the cage going to get the crat?"

"Who knows?" Weyr said. He laughed in delight. "That's the beauty of it. Almost anything can happen. That green could just sit there for the whole race. Salam are ornery that way."

Two slightly smaller salam, one brown with a long scar on its left shoulder, the other yellow-green, reared up onto their hind legs. They clawed each other. Weyr leaned forward eagerly to watch them. The yellow-green lizard took a slight step backward. Weyr remembered the brown salam he had seen in the ditch the day he had joined the Agari party. His stomach fluttered. Yes!

"Half a copper on the brown to dominate, even money," Weyr shouted.

"Covered." Weyr saw a squat Tamish man across the field wave at him.

"What did you do?" Kamlar said.

"I bet that the brown lizard will dominate the yellow-green he's fighting with."

"Kill him?"

"Not kill. They don't usually kill each other," Weyr said. "I just bet that the brown will drive the other one away."

"What made you decide to bet on that particular one?" Kamlar said.

"I don't know," Weyr said. He did not want to admit he believed in salam omens. Besides, Kamlar would not understand that. "I just had a hunch. I liked the looks of him. He seems as though he'll be a scrapper."

Two other salam reared up to fight on the opposite side of the field. Several people called bets on the fight. Weyr looked at the other lizards for a moment. He felt a pang of irritation at himself for being so easily distracted. But there was so much to watch at a salam race. He turned back to the brown salam he had bet on.

The brown nipped at the neck of its yellow-green opponent. The yellow-green swayed for a moment, then abruptly dropped to all four feet and retreated toward the side of the field.

"Got him!" Weyr said. He slapped a fist into the palm of his hand.

The brown lizard, victorious, also dropped to all four feet. It stopped motionless for an instant and then scurried toward the reed crat cage. The insect moved to the opposite end of the small enclosure, whistling in agitation. The crowd quieted some. Weyr felt his breathing quicken.

The scarred brown salam's long tongue darted through an opening in the cage and neatly severed the insect. With two more strikes of its tongue the salam had swallowed the crat.

The spectators stamped their feet. There were loud cheers and equally loud groans. Weyr had had nothing at stake, but he stamped his feet and joined in the cheers anyway. It was good to hear the familiar sounds of a completed race.

"Crat kill to Garvel's brown." The starter, an old woman with gnarled hands and a scar on one cheek, chanted the ritual end to the race. "Pot goes to Garvel and her backers. Bettors pay off on the crat kill and all other bets. Next round after the sound of the bell."

The man who had waved to cover Weyr's bet flipped a coin across the salam field. Weyr caught it and bowed slightly toward the man. The man grinned and shrugged. Weyr grunted in satisfaction.

"Well, what do you think?" Weyr asked Kamlar.

Kamlar grinned. "I think Tam are just as noisy as Agari," he said.

Weyr laughed. "Only at salam races," he said. "Come on. Let's look at the racers for the next round."

There were eight entrants for the next race. The owners, three men and five women, crouched beside the traditional reed salam baskets. Weyr tried to affect the expected pose of casual interest as he peered into several of them. But he again felt a flutter in his stomach.

"Back the green for a copper?" one of the owners, a heavy-set middle-aged Tamish man, asked. "I'll give you three on one, a third back on the loss."

Weyr looked at the salam. Its scaly green body was perhaps five inches long, with another two inches of newly grown stubby tail. The regenerated tail was a hopeful sign. It meant the lizard was healthy and probably a good fighter. Bad fighters did not generally regenerate their tails.

"For a green, this one's a scrapper," the owner said. "Lost his tail to a bigger brown, but still made the kill."

"I'll back him for a copper at six on one, and half back, si'be," Weyr said.

"You think I'm running an asham?" the man said. "I'm not talking charity. I'm talking serious backing."

"You don't believe in your lizard?" Weyr said.

"I'll give you four on one, no more," the man said. "But it stays a third on the loss. Here, look at him."

The man knelt beside the caged lizard. His lips quivered as he imitated the high-pitched whistle of the crat. The salam in the cage whirled toward the sound. The man looked up at Weyr and Kamlar.

"Crat sensitive, this one is, you'd better believe," the man said. "He's made the kill three out of his last seven."

Weyr eyed the bright-green reptile for a moment more.

"Five on one and a third back," Weyr said.

"Four, and a third," the man said.

"Bad bet, no backing, si'be," Weyr said. He took a step away from the man.

"Five with a third, then," the man said. "You're a hard backer for one so young. Let's see your money."

Weyr smiled inwardly. Whatever else had happened during the time he had spent with the Agari, he hadn't lost his edge in salam betting. He handed the man a coin and turned away.

"Another copper toward the ante," the man shouted behind him.

"Covered," said several other voices.

Weyr led Kamlar back to the salam field. Valmo followed a few feet behind them.

"What did you do?" Kamlar said.

"I backed his lizard," Weyr said, "just for this one race. Now he can up the ante. If the other racers cover, or get someone to cover for them like I did for him, it'll be a bigger pot. Otherwise they have to drop out and lose the ante they've already put up."

"What happens if his salam wins?" Kamlar said.

"He'll pay me five to one on my copper. It's an eight-salam race, so he wins three on my backing," Weyr said. "If his lizard loses, he pays me a third. I lose two thirds."

Kamlar frowned, puzzled.

"I guess I get all that," Kamlar said. "But will he pay you? Will he remember you? You've never seen him before in your life. How do you know he's honest?"

Weyr stared at Kamlar in astonishment.

"Of course he'll pay," Weyr said. "Everyone pays on the salam."

"Oh," Kamlar said.

"Do you want to bet?" Weyr said.

"I wouldn't know how. Besides, my father . . ." Kamlar began. He paused, then grinned impishly. "You bet for me." He handed Weyr a coin.

"Want to back the green, like I did?" Weyr said.

"Why not?" Kamlar said.

Weyr had just time to place the bet with the owner of the green and scurry back to where Kamlar and Valmo waited beside the field before the starter rang a small metal bell for the next race. Owners crouched behind the walls of the field, each with a salam basket. Several people called out bets.

The starter raised one gnarled hand and dropped it. "Salam open!" she cried. Weyr leaned forward in anticipation. Each owner dumped a salam onto the ground. The lizards scurried aimlessly. Weyr eyed the crat cage in the center of the field. The insect inside the cage moved around the enclosure. It made no sound.

"Stir the crat," Weyr said. "We've got a silent one."

"Right you are," the starter said.

The starter poked at the insect with a wooden pole. The crat began to whistle. Several salam, including the green Weyr had backed, turned toward the cage. The crowd cheered. Weyr joined the cheers for a moment. He heard more bets placed. His green approached within a few inches of the whistling crat in the cage and froze. Weyr cheered again.

For just an instant Weyr heard another whistling sound. The green lizard spun in its place. Two other salam stopped dead in their tracks. Weyr's jaw dropped open in astonishment.

"She cried crat!" a voice said. "I heard her. She cried crat!"

The owner of the salam Weyr had backed pointed at a husky Tam woman salam racer who crouched beside the wall across the field from him. The woman flinched.

"I did not!" the woman said in a hoarse voice. "He's lying. I did not cry crat."

The woman struggled to her feet. Several spectators gathered around her.

"It wasn't me," the woman said. "Someone else must have done it. Why would I cry crat?"

"We have an accusation of crat cry," said the starter. Her voice sounded both shocked and indignant. "Does anyone call witness?"

"I do," said one of the spectators who blocked the husky woman's way.

"And I," said another.

The accused woman tried to duck through the surrounding crowd of spectators. Someone threw her back. She landed heavily on her buttocks. The starter elbowed her way through the crowd.

"We have three witnesses to crat cry against the Lamva,

a Wayfarer," the starter said. "That is sufficient. Landon, Teglar, Belvor, take her. The rest of you stay clear. She will see proper judgment."

"It wasn't me. I tell you, it wasn't me," the woman said. "I would never, never . . ." Her voice trailed off in a whine.

Two women and a man lifted the accused woman to her feet and dragged her away. Others followed. They jeered and shook their fists. Weyr shouted a curse at the woman and turned to follow the crowd. Kamlar stood, open-mouthed, beside him. Valmo, the guard, had a hand on the hilt of his sword. Weyr stopped. He was not alone. He could not follow the others.

The man whose lizard Weyr had backed strode across the field, the basket containing his salam under his arm. He hastily handed Weyr two coins.

"Take your backing," the man said. "There'll be no more salam racing until she's found justice, the thieving daughter of a fox. What does she think, we're stupid as roqurs? May you find your Tranquility."

"And you, si'be. May you . . ." Weyr started automatically, but the man was already gone after the others.

Within a minute or two everyone had followed the shouting crowd. Weyr, Kamlar, and Valmo stood alone beside the salam field.

"By The Comet!" Kamlar said. "What did that woman do?"

"Do?" Weyr said. "What do you mean, what did she *do*? She cried crat, that's what she did!"

Kamlar stared at Weyr, his eyes wide. "You're really angry, aren't you, Weyr?" he said.

Weyr realized he had assumed a fighting posture. He was poised on the balls of his feet, his elbows tight to his side, his hands out, his fists clenched. Weyr took a deep breath and tried to relax.

"We'd better get back to my father's camp," Kamlar said.

They started out of the village. At first Weyr's knees felt a little shaky. Walking steadied them.

"Don't say anything if you're too upset," Kamlar said after a few minutes. "But can I ask you what 'crying crat' is?"

"I'm all right now," Weyr said. "'Crying crat' means imitating the sound the crat makes. That woman was trying to distract the lead salam."

"Would that make her salam win?"

"Not necessarily," Weyr said. "But it might keep the lead lizard from making crat kill. She must have thought no one would hear her in all the noise."

"So she cheated?" Kamlar said.

Weyr nodded.

"Does that happen often?" Kamlar said.

"I've never seen it. I've only heard stories about it," Weyr said. He shook his head. "Nobody cheats at salam."

Weyr heard angry crowd noises in the distance. He tried to send his extended senses in the direction of the sound, but nothing happened.

"What will they do to the woman?" Kamlar said.

"Lock her up, if she's lucky and the racers and bettors don't get at her first," Weyr said. "Then they'll probably make her pay a lot of money to the village, or maybe put her to working asham for a long time."

"I thought the asham was for poor people," Kamlar said.

"It's for criminals like her, too!" Weyr said. Involuntarily, his fists clenched again. Weyr flexed his fingers to relax them.

Kamlar shook his head in wonder. He was silent for a moment.

"When Agari want to tell you somebody is serious about gambling, they say 'He bets like a Tam,'" Kamlar said, his voice low. "Now I think I know what they mean."

"Well, what would Agari do with a filthy cheater?" Weyr said.

"I don't know. Nobody likes them very much," Kamlar said. "I guess if people found out about it, they'd make her pay back what she won by cheating and wouldn't let her gamble again. But they wouldn't lock her up or take away a lot of her money."

"That's the Agari Way with cheaters?" Weyr said, incredulous. "They'd let somebody off that easily?"

"As far as I know," Kamlar said. "People don't talk a lot about it."

"That woman deserves whatever she's going to get, and more," Weyr said firmly. "Nobody cheats at salam. *Nobody.*"

"If you say so," Kamlar said.

Weyr shook his head. Kamlar obviously did not understand. The Agari Way about gambling was evidently quite different from the Tamish Way. Weyr had long since decided that the Agari were not witches. But some things about the Agari were surely very, very strange.

Chapter Eight

"No, I suppose Kamlar didn't understand," Relinda said.

As soon as he had returned to camp, Weyr had sought out Relinda to tell her about the woman who had cried crat at the salam race. Nomer came by as Weyr was telling Relinda the story.

"I got mad as an ab bull in rut. It was awful," Weyr said. "But it didn't seem to bother Kam at all."

"I can imagine," Relinda said. "I've only witnessed someone crying crat once or twice. People were furious. But you have to grow up with it to know how serious Tam are about their betting."

"Kill the bear, eh, Rel?" Nomer said.

Relinda laughed. Weyr frowned, puzzled at Nomer's non sequitur. Relinda smiled at Weyr. "That's a line from a joke the Agari around Domn tell about the Tam and their gambling," Relinda said.

"What's the joke?" Weyr said.

"An Agari hunter in the mountains is returning from

the hunt with only one arrow left for his bow," Relinda said. "He comes to the edge of a cliff and looks down."

By tiny movements of her head, Relinda suggested the hunter peering over the cliff.

"In a little valley below him, the hunter sees a Tamish man," Relinda said. "There's a bear coming at the Tamish man from one direction, a wolf coming at him from another direction, and a crazed ab bull coming at him from a third direction."

The timbre of Relinda's voice and her expression changed slightly as she named each animal, hinting at both the sound and the appearance of the creature. In spite of himself, Weyr smiled, fascinated by the subtle mimicry.

"'Quick!' the Agari hunter says to the Tamish man," Relinda said. "'I've got only one arrow, and then you're on your own. Which animal shall I kill?'" Relinda paused for an instant and then, in a different voice, imitated the Tamish man. "'Kill the bear,' the Tam says. 'I bet with the ab at two to one that the wolf will eat me alive.'"

Weyr guffawed, then shook his head in irritation at himself. The joke was funny. But he was not sure he liked the fact that it was an Agari joke about Tam. Even though Relinda had told the story, it irked him that Nomer had suggested the joke. Nomer probably didn't understand how important the incident at the salam race was any more than Kamlar.

"It was serious when that woman cried crat," Weyr said. He scowled at Nomer.

"No offense meant to you, Weyr. I know it was serious," Nomer said. "Honor at gambling touches the Tamish soul, eh? I've lived among Tam for the better part of twenty years, Weyr. I understand that. And I've bet salam more times than you have, I imagine."

"*You* bet salam?" Weyr said.

"Not so much anymore. Now I prefer other bets," Nomer said. "But the truth is that in this family I'm the one who's the gambler. Rel bets very little, at least for a Tam."

"I guess I don't bet a lot, either. For a Tam," Weyr said. Without thinking, he said, "Kam told me that about you, Nomer."

"Told you what?" Nomer said.

Weyr felt blood rush to his cheeks. He wished he could take back what he had just said. But there was nothing to do about it but to go ahead.

"Kam told me his father said that when it comes to betting, you're a little Tamish at heart," Weyr said sheepishly.

Nomer threw back his head and laughed his deep laugh.

"Lakren should know," Nomer said. "He accuses me of that every once in a while, and not just about gambling. He has for years. He may be right, at that. About gambling I'm more Tamish than Rel. And I'm probably Tamish in some other ways Lakren doesn't much understand."

Weyr did not know what Nomer meant, but he was too relieved by the fact that Nomer did not seem offended by his report of the Instrument's comments to ask for an explanation.

"Well, tomorrow, at least, Lakren will see the Agari side of you, Nomer," Relinda said. "And of me."

Weyr looked quizzically at Nomer and Relinda.

"We're going to do a small musical show for the Instru-

ment and his guards," Nomer said. "A command performance, you might say. Perhaps a little payment due on the
Instrument's protection." Weyr could not tell from Nomer's tone whether he was pleased or displeased. "It'll be all
Agari songs."

"Do you usually do Agari songs when you perform?"
Weyr asked.

"The truth is we do whatever will bring in a house,"
Nomer said, his tone slightly ironic. "We've worked a lot
of places. Up in the Agari part of the mountains, we did
Agari material, naturally. The past couple of years, we
worked the Mountain Tam areas, then the Fields, and
finally in and around Carda. So of course we did Tamish
material. But Lakren gets homesick for the sounds of his
childhood, and most of the guards know only one tongue.
Tomorrow it's all Agari."

"I'm just as happy," Relinda said. "I've missed performing the Agari repertoire."

Weyr raised his eyebrows. Relinda smiled.

"I love Agari music, Weyr," Relinda said. "I guess that's
one thing that makes me a little Agari at heart."

~

Later Nomer and Relinda went into the village. As they
had done several times before, they asked Weyr to look
after Berthin.

"I've got something to show you, Weyr," Berthin said
when her parents had left. "Turn around, close your eyes,
and don't open them until I tell you."

Weyr complied. For a few moments he heard rustling
sounds and an occasional giggle.

"No peeking," Berthin said.

"I wouldn't think of it," Weyr said.

There were more rustling sounds.

"You can look now," Berthin said.

Weyr blinked. Berthin had exchanged the plain brown Tamish tob and blav she usually wore for an ankle-length gown of the brightest orange cloth Weyr had ever seen. Green sequins dotted the cloth. Her braids were undone, and her blond hair hung down almost to her waist. Berthin turned slowly in a full circle. She was quite beautiful, Weyr thought.

"This is what I'm going to wear to the concert tomorrow," Berthin said. "Relinda made it for me. Do you like it?"

"It's very pretty," Weyr said. "It's Agari, isn't it?"

"Yes."

"I've never seen you wear Agari clothes before."

"Sometimes I dress like an Agari and sometimes I dress like a Tam," Berthin said.

"So which are you?" Weyr said in a teasing tone.

For an instant Weyr wondered if that was an appropriate subject to tease Berthin about. But she did not seem offended.

"Sometimes I'm a Tam and sometimes I'm an Agari," Berthin said, teasing back. "You have to guess which."

"I see."

Berthin's voice turned serious. "But really and truly I'm always both. I'm all mixed up together," she said. "Nomer and Relinda say that's the best way to be."

"Well, I like you whatever you are," Weyr said.

～

What he had told Berthin was true, Weyr thought as the little girl went back into the wagon to change her clothes. He had grown quite fond of her. But the conversations with Berthin and Nomer and Relinda puzzled him.

From his talks with Kamlar, he had begun to think that there were two ways of doing things, the Agari Way and the Tamish Way. Yet Relinda had told an Agari story that, while it was funny, also made the Tam seem a little ridiculous. Relinda was also, she said, a little "Agari at heart" about music. Nomer was "Tamish at heart," at least about gambling. And Berthin thought the best way to be was "all mixed up together."

Nomer, Relinda and Berthin followed neither the Agari Way nor the Tamish Way. Or they followed both.

Traveling with the Agari party, Weyr thought, seemed a good deal more complicated a matter than it had the day before.

~

Weyr spontaneously burst into applause when Nomer, Relinda, and Berthin emerged from their wagon the next evening.

Berthin was wearing her orange gown, but Nomer and Relinda were dressed in a way Weyr had never seen before.

Nomer's clothes had basically the same design as those he usually wore, a pair of trousers tied at the ankles and an open-necked shirt tucked in at the waist, this time both the same shade of bright red. But the cloth in the trousers and shirt had a sheen to it that made it look rich and elegant. Elaborate embroidered designs done in a slightly paler red ran through the material. The sleeves of the shirt ended in red lace. A long sash of vermilion cloth was wrapped several times around Nomer's waist and tied over his stomach. The ends reached almost to his knees.

Like Berthin, Relinda wore an ankle-length gown. Hers was made of dark-blue cloth rippled with intricate embroidered designs in gold and white. The gown was open at the neck, and it fit tightly so it accentuated her small breasts. Relinda's black hair reached almost to her waist. She wore large, dangling blue earrings made in a crescent shape. With a start, Weyr saw that Nomer also wore earrings. His were hoop-shaped and red. Weyr had never before seen a man wear earrings.

Nomer and Berthin bowed when Weyr applauded.

"A good sign when you get a hand before you even open your mouth," Nomer said.

Relinda smiled wryly. "If you're interested, Weyr, this is what Agari high fashion looks like," she said.

"Or what it looked like a couple of years ago, when we left Domn," Nomer said. "There aren't many who pay much attention to Agari fashions in Carda or in the back country."

"More's the pity," Relinda said.

"Can't wait to get back to a real city, eh, Rel?" Nomer said.

"Praise The Powers, it's coming soon," Relinda said.

Relinda carried a long-necked stringed instrument with a leather strap attached. The neck ended in a highly polished round wooden base that glistened in the fading sunlight. Weyr knew about and, in fact, had tried his hand at several Tamish stringed instruments, but he had not seen one like this before. He asked Relinda about it.

"It's called a lythe," Relinda said. "Many Agari performers use them. Near Domn even some Tam performers have taken them up."

Weyr followed Relinda, Nomer, and Berthin over to the main Agari camp. All of the Agari party, save for the inevitable two guards who kept watch, had gathered in front of a fire. Kamlar and the Instrument, it was clear, had, like Nomer and Relinda, dressed for the occasion. The Instrument's trousers and shirt were both purple, and the shirt had lace on the cuffs. Kamlar wore a shirt of mottled yellow and orange above deep red trousers. Each, like Nomer, had a sash of cloth wrapped around his waist. And each, like Nomer, wore earrings. For a moment, the elegant clothing made Weyr a little self-conscious about his plain brown-linen tob and blav.

Weyr settled onto the ground next to Kamlar. The guards who sat near them seemed unusually quiet, as if in anticipation. Nomer and Relinda stood on the opposite side of the fire, their faces brightly lit by the flickering flames. Relinda slipped the strap of the lythe over her shoulder, struck a chord on the strings, and immediately damped the sound with the palm of her hand.

"A-h-h-h-h-h."

Nomer's bass voice sounded softly in the low register and slowly moved upward. As it rose, it grew in volume until it reached a full-throated note high in the medium range. There it held. Nomer stood erect, his arms relaxed at his side. His red shirt fluttered at his stomach. Under his shaggy eyebrows his eyes glinted in the firelight. Relinda's rich low soprano began an octave above the note

Nomer had sung first, and eased upward, echoing Nomer. It held on the high note.

Nomer began a sliding, rippling sound that moved around, above, and below the note Relinda held, returned to it for a moment, then slipped away. Relinda again echoed Nomer's melody. Together they sang an intricate set of runs around the dominant note, sometimes in unison, more often in harmonies. The harmonies were open and fluid and never seemed to stay in quite the same place. There were no words, only the full and resonant sounds of the two voices flowing around each other.

The effect was like nothing Weyr had ever known. The music reminded him vaguely of some animal sound he thought he had once heard and could not place, but he knew that no animal could duplicate the complex harmonies and varied textures of the two intertwining voices. Goose bumps prickled along Weyr's back. Abruptly the sound stopped.

"What was that?" Weyr whispered to Kamlar.

"It's known as 'The Call,'" Kamlar said, also in a whisper. "It's very old. Most Agari singers begin a performance with it."

Relinda struck another chord on the lythe, and she and Nomer swung into one of the rollicking melodies they had sung on the road. Relinda kept up a complicated rhythm on the lythe. The Agari guards joined in the chorus. Weyr found he knew most of the words. He shook his head to clear it of the peculiar impression "The Call" had made on him and sang with them. Beside Weyr, Kamlar joined in, his treble off-key, and the Instrument droned behind them, but Weyr hardly noticed their discordant voices. He was simply pleased to sing.

For an hour or more Nomer and Relinda sang Agari songs, sometimes with the group, sometimes alone or as a pair. Although Weyr could recognize only a few words of most of them, from the tone of the melodies and the marvelously varied expressions on the faces of Nomer and Relinda as they sang, he thought he could guess what many of them were about. And Kamlar occasionally explained a song to Weyr. Some, like the one Nomer and Relinda had begun after "The Call," were the fast and playful tunes of the road. Others, Kamlar explained, were long ballads recounting Agari stories and history. The guards laughed and shouted at several of those. They were evidently funny. Still others, Weyr guessed from the way Nomer and Relinda sang them to each other, were love songs.

Despite the fact that he did not understand most of the words, Weyr was captivated by the music. He had heard Nomer and Relinda sing on the road. But that was nothing like this. On the road, Weyr thought, they had merely been singing. Here they were performing. There was a difference. He had never quite put the difference into words before, but he had felt it once or twice when he himself had prepared a Tamish song to sing at Festival in Bown. Then he had not merely sung. He had performed.

The music Nomer and Relinda made, separately and together, moved Weyr in a way he had been moved only a few times when he had heard professional Tamish musicians perform on Festival days or at the Grand Market. But Nomer and Relinda were far better than any of those musicians had been. They were simply beautiful. Weyr struggled to put a word to how the music made him feel about Nomer and Relinda. Finally it came to him. It was not a word he used often, but it was the right one. The word was *awe*. For the first time since he had known Nomer and Relinda, Weyr felt awed by them.

As the fire burned down, the songs changed. The music became quiet, plaintive, even melancholy. Nomer and Relinda's faces, barely visible now, were somber, their voices hushed. Relinda laid the lythe down, and they sang without accompaniment. The guards were quiet. Weyr found his mind drifting. He closed his eyes, let the sounds wash over him.

Odd, unrelated pictures came to Weyr. Slowly the pictures formed into an image of a wooded grove. The image was familiar. It was the southern grove he had seen when he had meditated just before meeting Kamlar. The trees had the same heart-shaped leaves of many shades of green and the same pale-white flowers and yellow oval fruits he had seen then. As he had that day, he sensed the syrupy smell of flowers and the sounds of insects and birds. Weyr heard again a regular pulsating roar of running water that he could not identify.

There was a new sound, too. He heard two voices, a man's and a woman's. The voices were singing. The song had a sweet but sad sound to it. In his mind Weyr moved across the grove toward the sound. He did not walk, precisely, but, in a way he did not understand, just moved. Weyr peered through a break in the heart-shaped leaves.

He was halfway up the side of a hill. In the distance, a red sun had begun to set on an enormous expanse of water. Below him, on a flat bluff above a cliff, was a small building, white against green foliage that surrounded it. A man and a woman sat on a stone bench in front of the building. Both wore white robes. They faced Weyr. The man had his arm around the woman's shoulder. They were too far away to see clearly, but Weyr thought that the man was a Tam and the woman an Agari. There was something odd about the man's appearance. Weyr looked more carefully and realized what it was. The man had only one arm. The sleeve of his robe on the side opposite the woman was knotted at the shoulder.

The man and the woman sang.

Their song drifted up to Weyr. Weyr was not sure whether or not there were words to the song. If there were, he could not understand them. The man's voice was as rich as Nomer's, but it was a tenor, not a bass, voice. The woman's voice was a clear, high soprano. In a dreamy way, Weyr knew that their voices, though different, were like Nomer's and Relinda's in their resonance and power. Although the melody was not the same, the song reminded Weyr of "The Call." The couple's music seemed almost an echo of Nomer and Relinda's.

The couple did not look upward in Weyr's direction, but Weyr felt that they were, somehow, singing to him. As he had done when Nomer and Relinda sang, Weyr let the music wash over him. The song ended. Weyr hesitated for a moment and then started down the hill toward the man and woman, again not walking, exactly, just moving.

The setting sun caught Weyr's eye. He watched it for a moment. Abruptly it disappeared. There was only a dull orange-and-red glow above the horizon. The glow darkened until it was almost gone. Weyr realized that he was staring into the dying embers of the Agari campfire. The Tamish man with the tenor voice and the Agari woman with the high soprano were gone. Dimly, Weyr remembered that he had heard the sound of applause. Nomer and Relinda stood silently, their hands clasped together, in the shadows just beyond the fire.

"Weyr? Weyr?" Kamlar's voice was quiet beside him. "Are you all right? It's over. The performance is over."

"I'm . . . all right. I'm fine," Weyr said. "I was . . . somewhere else."

"You certainly were," Kamlar said. "And I guess it's no wonder. Nomer and Relinda can do that. My father says they're the best singers — actors, too — he's ever heard. That's why he wanted to bring them back to Domn."

"They're the best singers I've ever heard, too," Weyr said. "They're somewhere."

"What?" Kamlar said. "Who are somewhere?"

"Nothing," Weyr said. He shook his head to clear it. "I guess I was just thinking about something else. But you're right about Nomer and Relinda."

As he walked back to Nomer and Relinda's wagon, Weyr felt an ache, almost like hunger. He wanted something, but he was not sure what he wanted. He had felt that ache before. It had come to him when he had had the earlier southern vision. But there had been no people in that vision, and no songs.

With a slight shiver, Weyr remembered the eerie effect of the melody Kamlar had said was known as "The Call." Why was it named "The Call"? Who was calling? And who was the melody calling to?

The Tamish man and Agari woman in his vision had sung. Somehow their voices and the voices of Nomer and Relinda had merged in his mind. Was their song a call, too? Could it be that they were calling to him, beckoning him, inviting him to join them? But if they were, who were they? Where would he join them? And why? And how?

Weyr fell asleep wondering who and where and why and how.

Chapter Nine

T HE MURMUR OF Nomer's voice, low but persistent, filtered into Weyr's mind. He turned in his bedroll toward the sound and half opened his eyes. The sun was barely up. Nomer sat cross-legged on the ground in front of the cooking fire. Relinda and Berthin were still asleep, wrapped in their blankets. A sheaf of paper, bound together at the edges, lay open on Nomer's lap. He was quietly reading aloud.

Weyr drifted halfway between sleep and wakefulness, lulled by the sound of Nomer's voice. A gleam of light caught his eye. Nomer had one elbow propped up on the tongue of the wagon so his forearm stood vertical with the palm of his hand toward Weyr. He held a coin between his fingers. Sunlight glinted against it. Nomer dipped his hand downward, then twisted it to its original position, palm forward. The coin was gone. Nomer dipped his hand again. The coin reappeared. Nomer moved his hand down and up several more times. Sometimes the coin was there. Sometimes it wasn't.

It was a magic trick, of course. But the magicians Weyr had seen perform similar tricks generally made a great show of it. Nomer did not appear to be much aware of what he was doing with the coin. Through all the movements of his hand, he continued to read quietly to himself. Idly, Weyr wondered how Nomer made the coin appear and disappear.

Weyr let his eyes drift shut again. He could still see Nomer's hand and the coin. Weyr smiled dreamily. Perhaps he could use his extended sight to find out how Nomer did the trick.

His eyes still closed, Weyr examined Nomer's movements. He found that he could place his sight so he could watch Nomer's hand either from in front or in back, as he chose. After a few moments of watching from several vantage points, he had the answer.

With his palm forward, Nomer gripped the coin between his forefinger and little finger, leaning it against his middle fingers, so it was showing. As Nomer dipped his wrist, he used his two middle fingers to pivot the coin, then placed them in front of it. The coin seemed to disappear, although it was, in fact, now at the back of Nomer's hand, still gripped between his forefinger and little finger. A reverse movement made the coin visible. The net effect was that Nomer could show either side of his hand with or without the coin being visible. Nomer's dexterity with his fingers was amazing, but the idea of the trick was simple.

"So that's how it's done," Weyr said quietly to himself.

"What?" Nomer said loudly. He sounded startled.

Weyr opened his eyes to see Nomer looking at him.

"Oh, good morning," Nomer said. "You're awake early."

"Good morning," Weyr said.

Weyr looked at Nomer and shook his head. Now he could see Nomer's hand only in the normal way. Weyr rubbed his eyes with his fingers, as he often did when he woke up, and closed his eyes, but he saw only blackness. His extended sight was gone. But he had been able to control the sight for a few minutes. He had never been able to do that before.

"So that's how *what* is done?" Nomer said.

Weyr felt a knot in his stomach. There was no way he could have discovered the secret of the trick without his extended sight, Weyr knew, but he could not tell Nomer that. Nomer arched his eyebrows in curiosity. He had to answer Nomer's question.

"How you perform the trick with the coin," Weyr said reluctantly.

"Oh," Nomer said. He tilted his head in puzzlement, then glanced at the coin in his hand and chuckled. "I was doing that, wasn't I? I guess I wasn't paying much attention. I was really concentrating on something else. But you do have to keep in practice, you know. So, how is it done?"

"You rotate the coin with your middle fingers so it's always on the opposite side of your hand from the person who's looking at you. If you want to make the coin look like it's disappeared, that is," Weyr said.

"You could see me do that?" Nomer said.

"I have very sharp eyes," Weyr said. His stomach knotted again.

"So you told me," Nomer said. His brown eyebrows furrowed. "I've never met anyone, though, except another professional magician, who could see it. You see quite a lot, don't you?"

"I guess." Weyr squirmed uncomfortably. He searched for a way to change the subject. "You said you have to keep in practice. What are you practicing for?"

"Rel and I are going to do a show in Warn," Nomer said. "That's a town several days up the road, into the Hills of Karmon. Lakren sent one of his men ahead to arrange it, which was very kind of him. We can use a booking."

"A magic show?"

"Some magic. Some singing."

"Singing like you did last night?" Weyr asked. The awe he had felt the previous evening returned to him. He said in a low voice, "That was beautiful."

"Thank you, Weyr. I take that as a real compliment. You seem to have a good musical ear," Nomer said. He hesitated a moment, then raised an eyebrow and said, "Maybe I shouldn't tell you this, but you also have a good voice. And that's a professional judgment."

Weyr felt blood run to his cheeks. It had not occurred to him that Nomer might have noticed his singing.

"I just like to sing," Weyr said.

"So you should," Nomer said. He paused a moment. Weyr had the feeling that Nomer was aware of his embarrassment. "But to answer your question, yes, we will be doing some singing in Warn. Tamish songs this time. It'll be a Tamish audience there. We'll probably do a scene or two from a play as well. Rel and I both prefer that, at least to the magic. I'm a magician only when I have to be."

"You said that once before," Weyr said. "What do you mean, 'have to be'?"

"'Have to be' means we need the money. Rel and I are really actors. But in the small towns you can't do just that, particularly with only two performers. People want a mixed show — magic, music, drama, a little of everything. That's what Rel and I have been doing for a living for a while now."

"Berthin said you were going to Domn to be actors — she said 'witches.'"

"That's Berth's little joke. We are going to be actors. Domn's the best theatre town north of Keytho. We've got a good booking in Domn. We . . . we used to play there a lot." A pained expression crossed Nomer's face and was gone. He pointed at the paper on his lap. "That's what I was doing. This is a script for a play Rel and I are going to do in Domn. Rel has been pushing me to get off book."

"Get off book?"

"Memorize my lines, so I don't have to rely on the 'book,' the script. Rel wants to start some preliminary rehearsals. She's a quicker study than I am. She's got most of her part down. I guess I've been pretty lazy about mine on this trip so far. So I'm working before she gets up."

"What's the play?" Weyr asked.

"It's called *The Peacemaker*. It's a new play by a woman named Damyn. She's one of Domn's more talented younger playwrights. It's about a man named Tano and his sister, Semala. Maybe you know the names?"

Tano and Semala sounded familiar. Weyr thought for a moment. He had heard the names in tales told by storytellers at the Grand Market, but he could not remember much about them.

"Tano was a prince, wasn't he?" Weyr said. "A long time ago."

"A prince of Domn. Later a king of Domn," Nomer said. "Back in the days when Tam had such things as princes and kings."

"May I look at the book?" Weyr said. "I've never seen a script for a play."

"Of course."

Weyr slid out of his blankets, walked to Nomer's side, and peered at the papers. The book was written in Tam, though the handwriting was more elaborate than anything Weyr had seen before.

"'The journey, once begun, became no easy mount,'" Weyr read. "'It balked at human will. It bore no bridle well. I rode, but only sometimes reined.'" Weyr looked at Nomer. "Do you say that?"

"It's lines for a song I sing — or rather, Tano sings. I'll be playing Tano. Rel's doing Semala and directing," Nomer said. He looked at Weyr, a surprised expression on his face, as though something had just struck him. "You can read?"

"My gran taught me," Weyr said.

"It's not so usual for a boy from the country to be able to read," Nomer said. "Or even a lot of them in the city."

"Gran was a scribe. She kept the village records in Bown, where I grew up," Weyr said. "I had to read for her when her eyes got bad. I used to write for her some, too."

"You must miss your gran," Nomer said, his voice neutral.

Weyr paused. During all the days he had been with Nomer and Relinda, they had asked him almost nothing about his life before he had joined them. He felt a moment of resentment at Nomer for asking him now. Chagrined, Weyr put the thought aside. Nomer wasn't being nosy.

"I miss her some," Weyr said cautiously. "We didn't always get along."

"That happens," Nomer said, his voice still neutral. "With me it was my parents. We didn't get along so well, either. They didn't die, like your gran, though — at least not while I was a boy. I just left them."

"You ran away?" Weyr said.

"I ran away. I was about your age, maybe a little older."

"Where did you go? I mean, where were you and where did you go?" Weyr's face flushed. Nomer had not talked about his past, either, Weyr realized. Perhaps he should not ask questions. "I'm sorry. It's none of my affair."

"It's all right," Nomer said. "I grew up in Elubin. That's the Agari city in the mountains beyond Domn. We would have said Domn was down in a valley below Elubin, even if Domn is reasonably far up in the foothills."

"Isn't Elubin where the Instrument comes from? He's the 'Representative and Instrument in Domn of the Merchants of Elubin,'" Weyr said.

"Yes. The Instrument and I were . . . friends . . . when we were boys. At least as much friends as the son of a wealthy merchant, like his father, and the son of an apprentice blacksmith who never had the gumption, or maybe the talent, to set up his own shop, like my father, could be."

"Did the Instrument have anything to do with your running away?" Weyr said.

He again wondered if he should ask Nomer questions. But Nomer did not seem upset. Weyr decided it didn't matter. Nomer wanted to talk.

"I suppose, in a way, he did. By the time I was your age, I'd already gotten it into my head that I wanted to be an actor," Nomer said. "Lakren — he wasn't the Instrument then, just Lakren — had a similar idea. We used to talk about it."

Weyr raised his eyebrows, but did not speak. He heard a crat whistle nearby.

"Not that either of us knew much about it, of course," Nomer said. "We'd both seen some snippets from plays — part of the kind of mixed performance Rel and I are going to do in Warn. Then we saw one real play, done by a touring company that came through Elubin. It was a Tamish play. The Agari don't have much real theatre of their own. There are a lot of Agari performers — singers, storytellers, mimes and the like — but there's very little of what you can properly call theatre. This was a famous Tamish play, but performed in Agari. Lakren and I had to sneak in to see it, and both of our fathers beat us like we were rogue abs when they found out. But that made up my mind about being an actor."

"Did it make up the Instrument's mind, too?"

"Hardly." Nomer snorted. "In Lakren's case, his family had his life all planned out. I doubt that he was ever too serious about acting. He's ended up just about where his family intended — as a merchant and a diplomat. Though he's a generous patron of the theatre in Domn."

"But you ran away," Weyr said. "Where did you go?"

"At first I didn't know where I wanted to go, except that I had to get away from Elubin and I wanted to be an actor." Nomer's eyes focused somewhere beyond Weyr. "It was almost as if something was calling me."

A shiver ran down Weyr's spine. The sound of "The Call" echoed in his mind.

"For a while I just wandered, mostly to little places up in the mountains, working here and there at different jobs, performing where I could as a singer. I was a decent boy soprano, like you, and fortunately my voice stayed good when it changed. I learned some magic from an old traveling magician, and started performing as a magician sometimes, too," Nomer said. "I made up a lot of stories for people I met about where I was going. I don't know whether they believed them or not. Some people were nice." Nomer's face grew somber for a moment. "Some weren't. I got by. After a time I started hearing tales about Domn, about the theatres there."

"So you went to Domn?"

"Eventually, yes. I was awfully green, though." Nomer stared off into space for a moment. He looked pained. When he turned back to Weyr, his brows were furrowed in a sympathetic expression. "Domn's a very big place, Weyr. It can be pretty scary if you don't know your way around."

Weyr blinked, touched by Nomer's concern. He had not, he realized, really thought at all about what would happen to him when he reached Domn. In his whole life, he had never seen any town bigger than the villages along The Great Way. Suddenly the prospect of being all alone in a big city like Domn seemed daunting.

"I'll manage," Weyr said. He tried to make his voice sound confident, but he was not sure he had succeeded. Nomer was an actor, Weyr reminded himself. Actors knew about voices. "I'll get along fine in Domn."

"I'm sure you will," Nomer said. "But if you need help — of any kind — you just ask us."

Weyr nodded. "Thank you, Nomer," he said. "I will."

"In any case, you're lucky you have your cousin to go to," Nomer said.

Weyr glanced at Relinda and Berthin, still asleep near the wagon, and then back at Nomer.

"I am lucky," Weyr said.

Chapter Ten

WELL, THIS ISN'T getting my part learned," Nomer said. He looked at the papers on his lap, then back at Weyr. "Here's an idea. Since it turns out that you can read, would you help me run lines? You read the script, and I'll say my part. Correct me when I make a mistake. I'll tell you the story as we go along. All right?"

"That's fine," Weyr said.

For an hour or so, until Berthin and Relinda woke, Weyr helped Nomer rehearse. Nomer recited lines from the passage he had been reading, and Weyr, script in hand, followed along. The speech, or rather the speech and song — for Nomer often consulted another book, which had symbols Weyr could not read, and then softly sang the words — was, Nomer explained, the opening of the play.

Tano, Nomer said, had been born Prince of Domn, but he had left Domn when he was very young because Domn was often at war and he did not want to be a warrior. He had spent his life as a wanderer, a dreamer, a seer, a man who had tried to bring peace to warring Tamish peoples. Now he returned, unrecognized, to the city of his birth where his sister, Semala, ruled. He wanted to persuade Domn to make peace with the city of Rahv, its major enemy.

Tano sang and spoke about the many journeys that had finally led him back to Domn. He likened them to riding an animal that constantly changed from one creature to another. The beast was sometimes a horse, sometimes an ab, sometimes a braw or a dove. Tano sang and spoke, too, about his deep yearning for peace. The sentences Nomer had to say and sing were eloquent and, Weyr thought, complicated and hard to utter. Nomer insisted that he must learn every word precisely as it was written. He made frequent mistakes. Weyr corrected him, reading from the script.

Weyr rehearsed lines with Nomer twice more that day. By the last time, Weyr found that he did not have to look too much at the script to correct Nomer. He knew many of the lines by heart. In fact, he knew the lines better than Nomer did. Nomer stumbled over words and had Weyr repeat them to him many times. He was apologetic about that.

"I'm what they call in the theatre a slow study," Nomer said. "It takes me a long time to learn a part. My only redeeming virtue on that score is that once I've got a part, I never forget it. I can still do roles word for word that I learned ten or fifteen years ago and haven't played since."

The next morning Nomer woke Weyr early, and they worked on a scene from a different section of the script. In the new scene Nomer's character, Tano, proclaimed his mission of peace to the townspeople of Domn. The Domnish citizens were skeptical, even hostile, at first, and only at the end of the scene did Tano persuade them that peace might be possible.

To help Nomer learn his lines, Weyr quietly spoke the words of various townspeople as they appeared in the script. At first Weyr merely recited the townspeople's lines. After a few minutes he could not resist the urge to do more than that, and he tried out a different voice for one of the characters, imitating Anzia's rasping sound. Nomer did not say his next line. Instead he stopped and regarded Weyr quizzically.

"Whose voice was that?" Nomer said.

"I'm sorry," Weyr said, embarrassed. "I didn't mean to distract you."

"No, no, that's all right," Nomer said. "But that sounded like a real voice you were mimicking. Whose was it?"

"Someone named Anzia. I knew her in Bown."

"Can you do anyone else?" Nomer said. "Try to read the line in someone else's voice."

Weyr imitated Borno's harsh tones as he read the line again. Nomer raised his brown eyebrows. He pursed his lips.

"And sing, too," Nomer said.

"Beg pardon?" Weyr said.

"Nothing," Nomer said. "Do that some more. From now on, read the cue lines that way, with other voices. It'll be more interesting for both of us."

～

"Nomer tells me you've been helping him learn his part for *The Peacemaker*," Relinda said the next day. "How do you like acting?"

"I'm not really acting," Weyr said. "I just read the lines. But I like it. It's fun."

Relinda's mouth turned up in a half smile. "It's nice to be reminded of that," she said.

"Don't you have fun when you act?"

"Truth to tell, even after all these years, I do," Relinda said. "If I didn't think it was fun, at least most of the time, I guess I'd get into some other line of work."

"Have you been an actor all your life?"

"You could say that," Relinda said, "though it took me a while before I knew that's what I was. I had to leave Dalt — that's the little village where I grew up — to find out."

"Did you run away from home, like Nomer did?"

"Nomer told you about that?"

Weyr nodded.

"Well, in a sense I did run away, though not all by myself like Nomer," Relinda said. "A band of traveling entertainers came through Dalt, a Tamish man and woman and an Agari man and woman. Nomer was the Agari man. They were all on a barnstorming tour out from Domn. A lot of theatre people in Domn make their living that way when there's not much work in the city, though I didn't know that at the time. I had always liked to sing and dance, and I followed them around and pestered them until they finally let me perform for them. They said they liked what I did, but that I was too young and I should wait a few years."

"How old were you?"

"Sixteen. That was a long time ago."

"Did you wait?"

"Hardly," Relinda said. She gave a throaty laugh. "When the company left Dalt, I followed them for a couple of days without letting them see me. At last I got up the courage to talk to them. I guess they figured that if I'd followed them that far, I was serious about performing. They let me stay with them. I worked with them for two seasons until the company broke up. Eventually Nomer and I were married."

"And you've been actors together ever since?"

"Mostly together, though in the early years we sometimes had to take separate parts," Relinda said. She cocked her head and looked at Weyr. "Nomer also tells me you have a good ear for voices."

Weyr shrugged, a bit embarrassed at the compliment. "I just like to imitate people," he said.

"Would you do a voice for me?"

Weyr said a line from *The Peacemaker* in Anzia's grating tones.

"Try another person," Relinda said.

Weyr used Borno's voice. Relinda pursed her lips in approval.

"Good," she said. "Try this. Laugh for me. Not your own laugh. Someone else's."

On impulse, Weyr imitated the Instrument's peculiar hooting laugh. Relinda had to pause for a moment to control her own laughter.

"That's very funny, Weyr," Relinda said. "Don't let Lakren hear you do it, though. The Instrument has a sense of humor about himself, but it has its limits."

Relinda paused for a moment, then nodded, as though she had decided something.

"Nomer and I want to run through the recognition scene of *The Peacemaker* tomorrow morning," Relinda said. "Nomer has had that part down for a while. It takes place in a prison. There's a small third part, a jailer. Do you think you could learn the part and help out by doing it with us tomorrow morning?"

"Could I!" Weyr said.

~

Weyr made an excuse to Kamlar for missing their usual evening game of shan and read the scene several times by the light of Nomer and Relinda's fire. As Weyr read the script, he remembered more of the story he had heard told by the storyteller at the Grand Market.

The recognition scene was the first face-to-face meeting between Tano, the Peacemaker, and his sister, Semala, the warrior Queen of Domn. Tano had tried to keep his real identity secret. He feared that Semala, who was powerful and ambitious, would think his mission of peace was a subterfuge to allow him to wrest power from her and take his place as King of Domn. Semala did not at first know her brother. Fearful of the support Tano had gained among the citizens of Domn, Semala had had Tano imprisoned. Now, in this scene, she visited him in his jail cell and recognized her brother by a birthmark.

Tano and Semala spoke and sang of their love for each other as children. They spoke, too, of Tano's mission to urge the citizens of Domn to lay down their arms and make peace. As Tano had feared, Semala accused him of treason. She begged him in the name of their childhood love and in the interests of the city of Domn to abandon his mission and return to his life as a wanderer and seer. Tano refused. The scene ended with Tano and Semala singing an anguished duet about the conflict between them. One would win and one would lose. There could be no reconciliation.

The jailer, which was the part Weyr was to read, was a slow-witted woman who spoke a few lines at the beginning of the scene and then listened to Tano and Semala's meeting. Weyr thought for a few minutes about whose voice he could use for the character. He snorted as an idea came to him. He would imitate Gran. Whose voice could be better for a jailer? Weyr quietly read the part to himself in Gran's crackling tones. By the time he had read it a few times, he knew the jailer's lines by heart.

∼

The next morning Weyr followed Nomer and Relinda to a spot at the bottom of a hill a short distance from the Agari camp, where they could still see Berthin, who slept beside their wagon, but would not disturb her. Relinda introduced Weyr to what she called "warm-ups" — stretching exercises and a series of nonsense sounds and musical scales — which Weyr imitated as well as he could. Then she and Nomer began the recognition scene.

Something of the awe Weyr had felt when he had heard Nomer and Relinda sing for the Instrument's party returned to him as they performed the scene. Weyr was fascinated by the range of Nomer and Relinda's voices and by the way in which they could, apparently at will, alter not only their facial expressions but the whole set of their bodies. Seeing them, Weyr could almost believe that they were Tano and Semala, people in a story that had taken place long ago in a city he had never seen. Weyr was so captivated by Nomer and Relinda that once when he was supposed to speak one of the jailer's lines, he completely forgot to do it.

"That's your cue, Weyr," Relinda said.

Hastily Weyr said the line in Gran's crackling voice. Nomer and Relinda continued. Weyr forgot his awe of them as he concentrated on remembering when he was supposed to speak. He made no more mistakes.

They rehearsed parts of the scene several more times, and the whole scene twice. Each time they paused, Nomer and Relinda discussed how the scene might be acted better. More accurately, Relinda gave instructions about the acting and Nomer followed them. When Relinda gave instructions, there was a crisp authority in her voice that Weyr had not heard before. Relinda also made several suggestions to Weyr about how he might say his few lines. Weyr did his best to follow them.

"I liked the voice you did for your jailer character," Relinda said during one break. "Is it modeled on someone you know?"

"Someone I used to know," Weyr said. "My gran."

Nomer raised an eyebrow. "Well, you seem to have put her to at least one good use," he said. "She makes a fine jailer."

The hint of a wry smile curled up one corner of Nomer's

mouth. Berthin had once said that her father knew all kinds of things about people, Weyr remembered. Berthin had been teasing, Weyr knew, but in a way she was right. He had said very little to Nomer about Gran. And yet Weyr had the feeling that Nomer understood much more than Weyr had told him.

"There's an old saw in the theatre about how an actor creates a character onstage," Nomer said. "It says, 'We mold the characters of the present out of the passions of the past.'"

He knew nothing about acting or about creating a character onstage, Weyr thought. But he did know how he felt about Gran. Gran had not been dead for long. Yet each time he had thought about her since he had joined the Agari party, she seemed farther and farther away. The years he had spent with Gran were beginning more and more to feel like part of a distant past. It was a comforting thought.

"Well, let's play the scene once more and call it a morning," Relinda said. "We've been at it quite a while."

Weyr looked at the sun, now well up on the horizon, and blinked in surprise. He had not realized how long they had rehearsed. He had been concentrating intensely. After his first awe and fascination with Nomer and Relinda had subsided, he had focused entirely on the rehearsal and his part in it. Not another thought had entered his head. And yet he had felt relaxed and easy during the entire time.

They began the recognition scene again. Weyr said his lines, then crouched down behind Nomer and Relinda as they started their duet. His part of the scene was finished. But the state of relaxed concentration he had felt most of the morning was still with him.

Weyr's mind drifted. An amusing idea struck him. What would it be like to see the recognition scene as an audience might view it? Weyr picked a spot fifty or so feet up the hill. Suppose he was there. What would the scene look like?

Weyr closed his eyes. Immediately he saw Nomer and Relinda below him, their arms around each other. Behind them a small figure crouched. Sounds echoed up the hill. Nomer's bass and Relinda's low soprano blended together for a moment, separated in aching unresolved harmonies, blended again. A shiver ran down Weyr's spine. The couple sang more. At last their voices rose to a final chord. As the chord ended, the picture and the sound in Weyr's mind faded. He opened his eyes.

Weyr shook his head, bewildered. How had he done that? For the second time in a few days — once with Nomer's coin trick and again today — he had quite deliberately placed the senses where he wanted them to be. What was happening to him?

Weyr closed his eyes and tried to will his sight and hearing up to the spot on the hill. He saw and heard nothing. After a moment, Weyr abandoned the effort. Willing the senses to move was evidently the wrong way to make them work. What was the right way? How had he done it? Weyr tried to recapture the feeling that had come over him just before he had sent the senses to the spot on the hill, but it eluded him. He did not know the right way. Still, somehow, the right way had come to him twice now. Perhaps it would come again.

He would have to wait.

Weyr fell in step with Nomer and Relinda as they started back up toward their wagon.

"It's nice to get back into the rhythm of a real rehearsal for a real show again, eh, Rel?" Nomer said.

"It was a good morning," Relinda said.

"How did you like it, Weyr?" Nomer asked.

"It was a good morning for me, too," Weyr said.

Chapter Eleven

"WHAT WERE YOU doing last night when you couldn't play shan?" Kamlar asked Weyr when they stopped to eat their midday meal. The other boy looked at his feet. "Don't tell me if it's none of my affair."

"It's all right," Weyr said. "I was reading a script so I could rehearse a scene with Nomer and Relinda this morning."

"You're rehearsing with them?" Kamlar said. He sounded astonished. "I knew you were a good singer, but I didn't know that you could act, too."

"I can't act," Weyr said. "I'm just reading the script with them to help them learn their parts. It's a play they're going to put on when they get to Domn."

"My father told me he was bringing them back to Domn so they could act in the theatre there again," Kamlar said. "I didn't realize that they had already decided which play they were going to do, though." He thought for a moment. "I'll bet it's my father's doing. My father must have brought that script with him from Domn for them. He's a big supporter of the theatre in Domn, you know."

"Nomer told me that."

"What do you do when you rehearse with Nomer and Relinda?"

"Mostly I read the script while Nomer says his lines and correct him if he makes a mistake. Today I read the part for a third character in a scene while Nomer and Relinda acted their parts."

"Tell me a line from your part," Kamlar said.

Weyr recited one of the jailer's lines in Gran's cracked voice.

"You *can* act!" Kamlar said.

"I don't know anything about acting," Weyr said. "I've only seen plays a few times in my life. I just like to imitate people sometimes."

"That's part of acting, isn't it?" Kamlar said. "Anyhow, I don't think Nomer and Relinda would let anyone rehearse with them who didn't have some talent. They're famous in Domn, you know. They were the best-known actor and actress in the theatre there." Kamlar's eyes flashed. "Wouldn't you like to perform with them?"

"I don't know," Weyr said. "I never thought about it. Would you?"

"Wouldn't I! Not that I have any talent that way," Kamlar said. His face took on a wistful expression. "You're lucky to be working with Nomer and Relinda, Weyr."

~

Weyr did not doubt that what Kamlar had said about Nomer and Relinda being famous in Domn was true, but he found the idea a little hard to put together with what he knew about them. He had never met people who were considered famous, but he had seen at a distance in the Grand Market a strange bald-headed Tamish man who, people said, was a well-known seer and soothsayer, and a tall, angular woman who was a Great Merchant from Carda. Both had seemed distant and austere. Nomer and Relinda were not that way. It was hard to reconcile Nomer's gentle, teasing ways, or Relinda's generosity and kindness toward him, with that idea of famous people. Nomer and Relinda were, well, just Nomer and Relinda.

Still, Weyr thought, he had been awed when Nomer and Relinda had sung for the Instrument and when they had first rehearsed the recognition scene. Nomer and Relinda were much, much better than any of the professional actors and singers Weyr had seen at the Grand Market. The idea that he might perform with them was ridiculous.

And yet. . . .

Despite himself, Weyr became intrigued by the notion. The memory of his few singing performances in Bown was bittersweet. The occasions had been among the few times when Weyr had really felt as though people in Bown might accept him. Some adults in the village — not Gran, naturally — had praised his singing. He had felt good, almost as though he belonged. The feeling had not lasted long, but he remembered it with some warmth. Performing again — and particularly performing with Nomer and Relinda — was pleasant to think about.

Weyr resolutely put the idea out of his mind. He was happy enough simply rehearsing *The Peacemaker* with Nomer and Relinda. There was plenty to do. Weyr took time to read the entire script through several times, until he had committed much of it to memory. He rehearsed the recognition scene and several other scenes with Nomer and Relinda, reading different roles.

Weyr worked hard at the rehearsals. Once or twice he tried to see if he could again use his extended senses to watch, but he was never able quite to regain the state of mind that had allowed him to do it. That did not seem too important. The concentrated effort of rehearsing was very satisfying. That was enough.

And yet, Weyr had to admit to himself, he was both pleased and flattered when Nomer and Relinda did, in fact, ask him to perform with them.

"How would you like to do a walk-on in the show Nomer and I are going to give in Warn?" Relinda asked Weyr one morning, after they had rehearsed a scene from *The Peacemaker*.

"What's a walk-on?"

"A small part," Relinda said. "You'd just come on a few times for a minute or two, to help us with props during the magic show."

"What are props?"

"Properties. The equipment we use," Nomer said. "You could also help backstage. It's always a bit hectic there for us during a show, and Berth is really too young to do much."

"We've been working you pretty hard in rehearsals," Relinda said. "We thought you might enjoy trying your hand in a real performance."

"I'd like that," Weyr said. "I don't know whether I could learn what to do, though."

"You've learned a lot of *The Peacemaker*," Nomer said. "You should be able to pick up a stagehand part pretty quickly. Maybe I can even teach you a little magic."

Weyr remembered the wistful expression on Kamlar's face when Kamlar had asked him if he had ever imagined performing with Nomer and Relinda.

"There's something else . . ." Weyr said.

"What is it, Weyr?" Relinda said.

"Well . . . could Kam help in some way, too, if he wants to?" Weyr said. "I think he might like that."

Nomer and Relinda exchanged glances.

"I can understand why you'd want your friend to do this with you, Weyr," Relinda said. "And I can understand why you think Kamlar might also like to try his hand at something theatrical." Relinda's voice took on a wry tone. "But I doubt that Kamlar's father would be too enthusiastic about the idea. Much as the Instrument enjoys being a patron of the theatre in Domn, I'm not sure how he'd take to his only son and heir being a stagehand and bit-part player."

It had not occurred to Weyr that Kamlar would have to get his father's permission to do anything like the work he was doing with Nomer and Relinda. But it was undoubtedly true.

"I hadn't thought of that," Weyr said.

"I'm not sure that Lakren would be opposed," Nomer said thoughtfully. "I think perhaps he brought Kamlar along on this trip so the boy would have a chance to spread his wings a bit. Lakren might view this as one such chance. And after all, he was more than a little stagestruck himself when he was Kamlar's age. What do you think, Rel? You're the boss. I could talk with Lakren."

"Yes, I suppose we could fit Kamlar in, too," Relinda said. "All right, Weyr, why don't you ask Kamlar if he wants to do this? Tell him it won't be any big part, just helping out, but he's welcome to work with us. If he's interested, Nomer can talk to his father."

Weyr nodded. "I'll ask Kam right away," he said. "But I know what his answer will be."

"It'll probably mean having guards underfoot backstage during the show," Nomer said. He chuckled. "I guess they won't steal any trade secrets."

~

"You mean it?" Kamlar said.

"Not me," Weyr said. "Relinda told me I could ask you. It's all right with her, and I guess she kind of decides things like that for the two of them. It's all right with Nomer, too."

"I don't know if my father would let me do it," Kamlar said. He frowned.

"Nomer said he'd talk with him," Weyr said.

"If anyone can convince my father, it would be Nomer," Kamlar said. "They've been good friends for a long time, I guess."

"Nomer said that," Weyr said.

"I can't believe I might be able to be in some kind of performance with Nomer and Relinda," Kamlar said. His blue eyes glistened. "Thanks, Weyr. You're a good friend, too."

~

That day the country through which the Agari party traveled began to change. Grain fields still flanked both sides of the road, but low hills, some dotted with fruit trees and some flecked with scrub brush, became more common. Weyr could sometimes see the outlines of what he thought might be mountains in the distance ahead of them.

"We're just moving into the Hills of Karmon," Kamlar told Weyr when he asked about the change. "Another day or so and we'll really be into them. Domn is fairly high up, you know."

"How much farther to Domn?"

"Maybe a couple of ninedays," Kamlar said. "The Hills get to be rough country. Travel is slower."

In the evening they camped along a slow-moving stream on the edge of low hills. The night was cold. When Weyr rose to join Nomer and Relinda for their early-morning rehearsal the next day, he shivered in his linen blav. Relinda rummaged in their wagon and emerged with a woolen jacket.

Weyr was grateful for the warmth, but the jacket made him feel a little strange, too. It was blue and orange, brightly colored in the Agari fashion. When Weyr first pulled it on, he felt for a moment as though he had put on something more than just a new piece of clothing. A glance at his reflection in a small pond made by a backwater in the stream confirmed the impression. Weyr's brown skin and broad, flat nose marked him as Tam, but with the coat he could easily be mistaken at a distance for an Agari. Weyr was not sure he liked the effect.

As Weyr and Kamlar went off to meditate after the

rehearsal, Nomer disappeared in the direction of the Instrument's tent. He returned just as Weyr came back alone to the wagon. Nomer nodded to Weyr and Relinda.

"It's all set for Kamlar to be part of the show," Nomer said. "You should be the one to ask the boy, Rel."

"I will," Relinda said.

"We can do some of the preliminary work tonight after we stop," Nomer said.

~

Two Agari guards hovered nearby that evening after dinner when Kamlar came by Nomer and Relinda's wagon, and he and Weyr began to learn what they were to do in the show in Warn. The show, Relinda said, would begin in late afternoon. After a few songs, she and Nomer would do magic while there was still natural light. A part of a play and more songs would follow as the evening came on and they performed by torchlight. Most of Weyr and Kamlar's work would be to prepare and give to Nomer and Relinda a number of props for the magic show.

"Tonight we'll just run through the props, so you get to know them," Nomer said.

From the wagon Nomer brought several crates of equipment. There were small boxes of various shapes, including one that looked empty at first but which, when Nomer touched a hidden lever on its side, suddenly filled with cloth flowers. There was a small table with a hidden compartment in it. The compartment would, Nomer assured Weyr and Kamlar, hold any small object up to and including a live salam. There were seemingly empty tubes from which Nomer produced scarfs and other objects, and many other items. The display was both bewildering and intriguing. Weyr was fascinated. Kamlar obviously was, too. Even Berthin, who, Weyr supposed, must have seen the equipment many times, watched Nomer's antics with some interest.

The most fascinating prop was a gaudy red-and-yellow cube-shaped wooden box perhaps two and a half or three feet on a side. Nomer helped Relinda crawl into it and then folded a hinged top with a hole in the middle over her so that only her head showed. From another crate he drew a large sword. Nomer flexed the blade. With a flourish he held up an orange scarf and sliced it in two with the sword. Then, grunting as though his work took great effort and uttering menacing growls, Nomer slowly drove the sword into a hole in the side of the box. Relinda writhed and screamed. The blade emerged on the opposite side. As far as Weyr could see, Nomer had driven the sword through Relinda.

Nomer drove a second sword through Relinda and then more swords, until there were five. Each time, he growled and Relinda moaned. As if on sudden inspiration, Nomer borrowed the sword of one of the Agari guards. The guard, who looked both bemused and astonished, watched as Nomer drove that sword, too, in near the others. Relinda now seemed to be impaled with six swords. She ogled the protruding blades.

Nomer pulled the swords out one by one, tugging mightily at each as he removed it. Relinda winced each time. When Nomer had finished, he opened the hinged door, and Relinda gracefully stepped out. Weyr could not see so much as a scratch on her body or a rip in her clothing. Kamlar laughed nervously.

How did Nomer and Relinda do the trick? Obviously there was something peculiar about the box. But what? On impulse, Weyr tried to will his extended sight to a spot where he could look inside it. He saw nothing. Weyr smiled ruefully. That was not the right way to make the senses work. But there was obviously a simpler way to answer his question.

"So how did you do it?" Weyr asked.

Nomer chuckled. "I guess now that you're going to perform with us, I can reveal a few more trade secrets," he said.

Nomer displayed the box to them. Inside, there was a crossed pattern of grooved boards. Nomer inserted a sword in one of the holes he had used before. It slid neatly between two of the grooved boards and out the other side.

"The swords can't slip out of the grooves," Nomer said. "The 'victim' just has to fit around them. The real trick isn't the prop. It's the people. The magician has to make you believe he's really running those swords through and the person inside has to howl like a gored ab. Why don't you try it? Weyr, you can be the victim and Kamlar the magician."

Fitting in among the grooved boards was not as easy as Relinda had made it look, but Weyr managed to arrange himself around them so that Kamlar could put the hinged top down. Weyr eyed the first sword apprehensively as Kamlar, grunting noisily, began to push it through a hole, but he felt nothing. He moaned and winced in what he hoped was a persuasive fashion. Kamlar completed the trick with the rest of the swords. Nomer laughed. Weyr tried to suppress a grin as he climbed back onto the ground at the conclusion of the trick.

Berthin clapped and cheered. "You're a lot more fun when you do that than Nomer and Relinda are," she said to Weyr and Kamlar.

Nomer threw up his hands. "An actor's nightmare," he said. "I'm raising a child who's going to grow up to be a critic. Here, we'd better put the equipment away before you two completely upstage us."

Under Nomer's supervision, Kamlar and Weyr took the box apart and stored it in Nomer and Relinda's wagon. Disassembled, it took up only a small space.

"I've seen that trick more than once, but I didn't have any idea how it was done," Kamlar said to Weyr. He grinned. "I knew I was going to like this."

Chapter Twelve

WEYR SENSED A restlessness in Kamlar as they rode the next day. At first he attributed it to excitement about the rehearsal with Nomer and Relinda, but later Weyr had the sense that there was something else at work, too. Not only Kamlar seemed restless. Others in the party did, too. The terrain had changed more. They had left the Fields of Westum altogether and now rode through low hills covered with shrub brush and a few trees. Occasionally Weyr saw sheep grazing in the distance. With the change in terrain, the mood of the travelers had also subtly changed. Kamlar confirmed Weyr's impression.

"We're really into the Hills of Karmon now," Kamlar said. "This is the worst part of the trip. It can get a little dangerous. People aren't always friendly up here. There are even bandits sometimes."

"Like there were Tam spies in the Fields of Westum?" Weyr said, teasing.

Kamlar laughed for a moment, but then his face turned somber.

"No, this is more serious," Kamlar said. "Watch the guards."

The guards did seem more alert than they had in the Fields of Westum. There was very little of the bantering and shouting Weyr had become used to. The party's line of march, which had been casual, was now much more uniform, with the guards arranged two abreast in a precise order. When other travelers appeared on the road, the guards watched them carefully until they passed.

The guards seemed especially alert when Weyr and Kamlar joined the Instrument as he went into the market area of a village in the Hills. As they wandered among the stalls and carts, the guards kept a wary eye on the crowd.

The Instrument stopped at a cart filled with jewelry and bargained with the owner, a plump Tamish woman in her forties. The Instrument's manner was brusque and peremptory. When he finished his business and turned away, the woman jerked a thumb in his direction, then put her forefinger to her nostril in a rude and explicit gesture. Weyr gasped and looked at the guards. But apparently no one else in the Instrument's party had noticed.

As Weyr walked down the line of carts beside Kamlar and the Instrument, he kept an eye on the Tamish woman. She turned to the man who owned the cart next to hers and began an agitated conversation with him. Both of them pointed at the Agari party.

Weyr jumped. Although he was perhaps a hundred feet away from the Tamish man and woman, and the noise of the market crowd surrounded him, he could hear them talk. Somehow, with absolutely no intention on his part, his extended hearing had focused on the pair.

"Look at the great Agari leader!" the woman said scornfully. "The coward! Can't go anywhere without his little army. Typical of an Agari."

"Cowards and bullies, the Agari are," the man said. "And every year they push out a little farther into the Tamish lands."

"Don't they! In Domn there are so many of them, they have a whole section of the city to themselves. I saw it with my own eyes."

"I heard that some Tamish folk in Domn killed a few of them," the man said.

"That's true. And more power to the killers, I say."

"Did you see the Tam boy?" the man said. "Not even old enough to sire a babe, he is, and already he's hiding behind the guards, just like he was one of the Agari."

"There are a lot like him, too," the woman said. "Tamish in the body, they are, but Agari in the head. The Agari get them young and witch their minds. Then they're worse than the filthy Agari. Why, I know for a fact that . . ."

Weyr half turned in the direction of the Tamish man and woman, his arms tight against his side, his fists knotted. The woman's voice wavered and faded. Then it was gone. The man and the woman still talked, but Weyr could not hear them.

Weyr deliberately loosened his fists. There was no reason to be so angry. The man and woman did not understand. They were ignorant. They knew nothing about the Agari, nothing about him. Why should he pay any attention to them? Weyr took a deep breath and tried to force himself to relax. He told himself he should not be so upset. The man and woman, after all, had not *done* anything to him. He had only overheard a conversation. The hateful things they had said about him were only so many words.

But words could hurt, too.

~

"Weyr, I want you to know how pleased we are with the way you're handling *The Peacemaker*," Relinda said the next morning after they had rehearsed and Nomer had gone off to talk with the Instrument. "You're really a remarkably quick study. You pick things up as fast as many professional performers."

"I don't know about that," Weyr said. "It doesn't seem too hard to do."

"It's not all that easy, even for some people in the business," Relinda said. She smiled. "Agari performers are supposed to be better at it than Tam. I guess Nomer's the exception that proves the rule." Relinda's voice took on a bantering tone. She pointed at the jacket Weyr had donned against the morning's chill. "Maybe you have a little Agari in you. You almost look it in that jacket."

"I'm not Agari, I'm Tam!" Weyr said. He flushed, startled at the strength of his response. He had not intended to say anything like that.

Relinda's thick eyebrows arched in surprise.

"I'm sorry," Relinda said. "I didn't mean to offend you. Weyr, what's wrong?"

Weyr hesitated for a moment until he found a way to tell Relinda about what had happened to him the day before without talking about his extended senses.

"Yesterday I . . . well, I wasn't spying or anything, but I accidentally heard two Tamish villagers talking about me,"

Weyr said. "They called me names. They said I was just like the Agari."

"So! Even with children!" Relinda said angrily. She sighed. "That hurts, doesn't it?"

Weyr nodded. "I tried not to pay any attention," he said. He looked at Relinda. "Do you think I really *am* like the Agari?"

"I think you're very much a Tam," Relinda said. "No one who really knows you could doubt it. What makes you ask? Is it more than being called names?"

Weyr was silent for a moment. He fingered the brightly colored cloth of the Agari jacket.

"It's, well, I guess it's a lot of things," Weyr said slowly. Half-forgotten memories began to surface in his mind. "Things people said."

"What kind of things?"

"Oh, for example, Kam always talks about the Agari Way, as though I should learn it," Weyr said. "Once the Instrument said I played shan like an Agari. I felt a little odd when you told that Agari joke about the Tam and gambling. And now when you said I looked Agari in this jacket . . . well, I know you were teasing, but it made me feel strange."

Relinda's face turned pensive. She said gently, "Being more or less alone among so many Agari hasn't been all that easy for you, has it, Weyr? You seemed to be doing so well with it, I didn't pay enough attention. I should have been more observant."

Weyr was a little ashamed of his outburst now. "I like it, too, though," he said. "I mean, I like being with all of you a lot. But it's, well, confusing sometimes."

"I'm sure it is," Relinda said. "Perhaps Nomer and I shouldn't tease or make jokes about the Tam and the Agari. That's just part of our way of dealing with who we are, I guess. You have to laugh about it once in a while, or you'll cry."

"In Bown, where I grew up, people sometimes said I had Agari blood," Weyr said.

"And having Agari blood was, of course, a bad thing," Relinda said. "I'm sorry I teased you about that. Not that having Agari 'blood' matters at all about anything important."

"People in Bown used to say I was a witch," Weyr said. "They said I was a witch because I had Agari blood."

"What do you think it really was that made them say you were a witch?" Relinda's voice was quiet.

"I don't know all the reasons," Weyr said cautiously. "People didn't like me because I wasn't born in Bown. That was part of it. And they . . . they thought I could see things no one else could."

"Weyr's sharp eyes, eh?" Relinda said. Her brown face looked sad. "Bown sounds like Dalt, where I was born. If you're at all different from everyone else, they call you names. I've been called 'witch.' And worse."

"By Tam?"

"Yes, by Tam."

Weyr blinked. It had not occurred to him that Tam might regard Relinda in the same way they apparently regarded him.

"Did they call you names because you were with the Agari?"

"Yes, recently it's been because I was with Agari. But it

started even earlier, when I was growing up." Relinda looked pensive. "Perhaps then it was because I could sing and dance and do voices, could stir up people's feelings. I don't know. People like that, but they're afraid of it, too. It makes them uncomfortable. Not that the Agari are very different. When we toured up in the Agari areas in the mountains, I sometimes got called names there, too."

"By Agari."

"By Agari," Relinda said. She looked at Weyr with a half smile. "If you'd grown up in an Agari village and been different, Weyr, they would probably have said it was because you had Tamish blood. You might even have been called a witch. Some Agari people think the Tam are witches."

"That's very strange," Weyr said. He again fingered his Agari coat. "Relinda, why do the Tam and the Agari so dislike one another?"

"For lots of reasons," Relinda said. "And for no reason. There were wars. Agari killed Tam. Tam killed Agari. That was years ago, before I was born, but some people have long memories." Relinda sighed. "Nomer and I have felt the sting of those memories. People — both Agari and Tam — can be very unpleasant about a Tam-Agari couple. Recently we've been in Tamish areas, so we've felt the Tamish sting. Particularly Nomer."

"Do Tamish people call Nomer names too?"

"I daresay they do. Of course, Nomer doesn't look particularly Agari. He's tall, and he can pass for a light-skinned Tam. And generally with entertainers it doesn't matter quite so much. If you're an entertainer, people expect you to be different. They tolerate it, even in the little villages, so long as you're only there for a day or two. But sometimes it can be ugly."

Relinda's mobile face looked pained. She stared off into the distance for a moment, silent. A braw circled in the air far above them.

"I chose my life," Relinda said. "I wouldn't have it any other way. But Nomer and I are both glad we're going back to Domn."

"You and Nomer really like Domn," Weyr said.

Relinda smiled. "Domn's the place to be, if you're an actor, at least in the north away from Keytho. Nomer and I did well there. We were lucky, and — without being falsely modest — we were talented. It was a little rough at first, but eventually we got some fine roles. We had a good life."

"Then why didn't you . . ." Weyr bit back his question.

"Stay in Domn?" Relinda said. "It's all right to ask, Weyr."

Weyr nodded.

"Nomer and I got into some . . . trouble . . . in Domn. Political trouble. It's a long story." Relinda stared off into the distance again for a moment. "At any rate, we went back on the road. It seemed the wisest and safest thing to do."

"But now you're going to live in Domn again?" Weyr said.

"I hope so. The political situation has changed in Domn . . . we think. The Instrument claims that's true. And whatever his limitations, the Instrument is generally a shrewd judge of politics. That's his business. I don't mind the road too much, but the prejudice is wearing. And it gets a bit lonesome."

"There isn't so much . . . prejudice . . . in Domn?"

"It's better there. Even though Domn is basically Tamish, you don't meet the same kind of anti-Agari feeling in the city as you do in the country. Not that the feelings aren't there. We had to leave because of them." Again a pained expression crossed Relinda's face. "But in Domn you can find places where you can avoid them. People are more willing to accept differences. That's particularly true in the theatre. The Domnish theatre is mainly Tam, but it has a fair sprinkling of Agari actors and designers and so on. And theatre people don't care much what you are as long as you're talented."

Relinda stared into the distance again. The braw still circled above the Hills of Karmon.

"Domn is really home to us," Relinda said. "As much as any place is home."

Home. The word resonated in Weyr's mind. It was not a word he had used much. Was any place home to him? Bown had been, he supposed. He had lived most of his life there. But he had never felt he belonged in Bown. Even when he had lived there, he had not really thought of Bown as home. And he did not miss Bown at all.

An image of the man and the woman beckoning to him in his southern vision bubbled up in Weyr's mind. He had felt an ache, a longing. Was the ache a longing for home? Weyr wondered if the vision had come from somewhere near Domn. Domn, Relinda had said, was a city where people were willing to accept differences. He was certainly different from other people, Weyr thought. He was, perhaps, a witch. Would people in Domn accept a witch?

He had been silent for some moments. He looked at Relinda.

"What are you thinking about, Weyr?" Relinda said. "If you don't mind my asking."

"I was wondering whether Domn will be home to me, too," Weyr said.

Relinda smiled at him. It was a friendly smile, but at the same time there was a wistful look in Relinda's eyes.

"Domn's a fine city" was all Relinda said.

Chapter Thirteen

"WEYR, DO YOU know 'River Wide, Boatman Ride'?" Nomer asked. "It's a Tamish boating song."

It was just after the evening meal. Relinda and Nomer sat across the fire from Weyr. Berthin nodded drowsily beside them. Relinda's lythe was on her lap. She plucked at one of the strings to tune it.

"Yes," Weyr said. "People used to sing it in Bown."

"I thought you might have sung it, Bown being near the river," Nomer said. "Why don't you try it with Rel and me?"

"What do you want me to do?"

"I'll sing lead," Nomer said. "On the chorus Rel will pick up one harmony part. See if you can pick up another. I've heard you improvise harmony. I'd like to hear what 'River Wide, Boatman Ride' sounds like with a third voice."

"All right."

Relinda hit a loud chord on the lythe. Weyr blinked in surprise. In Bown, "River Wide, Boatman Ride" had usually been sung without instruments or with only a drum for background. But as Nomer started into the words of the first verse, Weyr decided he liked it with lythe accompaniment. The song was boisterous and somewhat bawdy. Nomer lined out a verse in a raucous voice. The Tamish melody sounded slightly strange to Weyr's ear. He had, he realized, become accustomed to the syncopated rhythms and plaintive melodies of Agari music.

When Relinda joined Nomer in harmony for the chorus, Weyr listened for a few beats, and then began to sing a different, complementary harmony. Finding the right harmony to a song was not a process Weyr could really explain, even to himself. When people sang, there simply were open spaces between the notes. He listened for the spaces and filled them with other notes. Sometimes the process was easy, sometimes hard. But he generally knew when he had done it right. Weyr listened to his treble with Nomer's bass and Relinda's low soprano as they sang. He liked the sound.

When they finished the song, Berthin, who had come awake, smiled dazzlingly at Weyr. Nomer and Relinda glanced at each other. Relinda nodded slightly.

"That sounds good with the treble voice," Nomer said. "Weyr, 'River Wide, Boatman Ride' is one of the songs Rel and I are going to do in Warn. Would you like to do it with us?"

"You mean sing with you for an audience?"

"Exactly. You could do that in addition to the magic show," Nomer said. "Have you ever sung before an audience?"

"Once or twice," Weyr said. "It was just for people from Bown."

"Did you like it?" Nomer said.

"I was a little scared," Weyr said. "But, yes, I liked it."

"Why not try it with us, then?" Nomer said. "We'll be opening the show in Warn with music. That's the best way to warm up a crowd. You could join us on that one number. We'll rehearse it between now and then, so you feel comfortable. How does that seem?"

"It seems fine," Weyr said.

The three of them sang "River Wide, Boatman Ride" through several more times. Occasionally Nomer interrupted to suggest variations in Weyr's harmonies. Each time, the sound seemed better when Weyr sang as Nomer directed. Once Nomer made a suggestion to Relinda as well. Weyr realized that he must have had a surprised expression on his face when Relinda looked at him and laughed.

"I may do the stage direction for this pair of performers, Weyr," Relinda said by way of explanation, "but Nomer's the one with the finer ear."

As they sang the song through yet another time, Kamlar came by to begin the evening's work with the props. He squatted beside the fire and listened. When Nomer, Relinda, and Weyr finished, he clapped enthusiastically.

"Your first applause as a performer on the road, Weyr," Nomer said, teasing. He turned to Kamlar. "Weyr's going to join us on that number in Warn, Kamlar."

Kamlar's blue eyes were wide as he looked at Weyr.

"That's wonderful," Kamlar said.

~

"See, I told you Nomer and Relinda thought you had talent, Weyr," Kamlar said a little later, when he and Weyr were alone for a moment.

"It's only the one song," Weyr said apologetically. "And it's a Tamish song. I grew up with it."

"By The Comet, Weyr!" Kamlar said. "Do you think I'm jealous because you're going to sing with Nomer and Relinda and I'm not?"

Weyr nodded sheepishly.

"That's ridiculous," Kamlar said. "I know I can't sing. Sometimes I wish I could, but I can't, and that's that. It's like my father says, 'Wolves who can't howl shouldn't run with the pack.' I'm happy for you that you're going to sing with them. I'm just pleased you got me into the show at all. Helping with the props and the magic is fine with me."

~

Learning what to do with the props for the magic show was not difficult, Weyr found, but it did require attention to detail. The props were to be used in a particular order, which had to be memorized. Space on the stage was limited, Nomer said. Items had to be carried on and off as quickly and efficiently as possible.

"Pacing is everything in a magic show," Nomer said. "If you lose the pace, you lose the audience."

"Is it a good stage in the theatre in Warn?" Kamlar asked. "My father says you've played there before."

"Stage? Theatre?" Nomer said. He clucked derisively. "There's no stage in Warn at all. What they call a 'theatre' is just an indentation in the hills with a place for people to sit and a fence to keep the nonpaying public out." Nomer pointed to the wagon. "There's our stage. The wagon opens up into a platform. It's too much trouble to set it up now, but you'll see how it works in Warn. If you're barnstorming the way Rel and I have been, you bring your stage with you."

At each rehearsal, Nomer marked off a "stage" area on the ground, and Weyr and Kamlar practiced placing the props in the correct order "backstage," bringing them on in the appropriate sequence and storing them after they were used. Weyr was pleased — and, he admitted to himself, a little relieved — to see that Kamlar quickly and easily learned what he was supposed to do. Since he was responsible for Kamlar's participation in the show, Weyr wanted him to do well.

Weyr also rehearsed "River Wide, Boatman Ride" with Nomer and Relinda. Nomer's frequent suggestions made his part sound better and better. Nomer and Relinda were also going to perform a scene from a Tamish play, but Weyr did not see them rehearse that part of the show. They had performed the scene many times before, Nomer said. He was of the opinion that another rehearsal would do nothing more than make them stale with the parts. Finally, the night before they were to arrive in Warn, Nomer ran through the entire sequence of Weyr and Kamlar's part of the magic show.

"That's it," Nomer said when they finished. "We'll do a full-scale rehearsal with the stage tomorrow after we get to Warn. You feel ready?"

"I guess so," Weyr said. "Yes, I feel ready."

"I do, too," Kamlar said.

But that night before he went to sleep, in his mind Weyr carefully ran through each step of the instructions Nomer had given him.

~

The Agari party arrived in Warn almost at sundown. Weyr got a brief impression of the town as they rode through it. Warn was nestled in a valley between high, rugged hills. It was big, Weyr thought, bigger than any of the villages he had encountered in the Fields of Westum.

"Warn is a major transit point between Domn and the Fields on this part of The Great Way," Kamlar said. "There are two or three other roads that lead into it from the mountains."

The streets of Warn were busy and crowded. Most of the faces in the crowds were Tamish, though Weyr spied an occasional light-skinned Agari dressed in brightly colored clothes. The Instrument's party camped on the outskirts of the town. Nomer waved in the direction of the area where the performance was to take place as they passed it just before they reached their camp, but Weyr did not actually see it until the next day.

Early in the morning, Weyr and Kamlar followed Nomer and Relinda's wagon to the performance area. Two of the Instrument's guards rode with them. One of them was Valmo. Weyr talked briefly with him in an odd mixture of Tamish words Valmo understood and the growing number of Agari words Weyr knew.

A nervous bald-headed man, short for a Tam, met Nomer and Relinda. He was, Nomer explained while Relinda talked with him, a local man who served as a manager for traveling shows when they came to Warn. Nomer and Relinda had worked with him before. The man led them all to the amphitheatre.

The amphitheatre had obviously been used often for performances. A gently sloping hill where many people could sit led down to a small flat expanse of land backed by dense shrub brush. A fence surrounded the entire space, except for the shrubs, which made a natural fence. All of the ground had been worn bare even of grass by the tread of many feet. There were heavy braziers placed throughout the area for lighting during the later part of the performance. Nomer and Relinda drew their wagon onto the flat land at the bottom of the hill and unhitched the horse. Valmo took the animal back to the nearby Agari camp and returned to stand guard.

Weyr and Kamlar helped Nomer remove the covering and ribbing from the wagon. Once the wagon's contents had been stored beneath and behind it, the flat bed of the wagon became an adequate, if small, stage. The brightly colored cloth that normally covered the wagon was hung from wooden uprights and cross beams fitted into slots in the bed of the wagon. It became a backdrop.

"That's 'backstage,'" Nomer said. He gestured at the area between the wagon and the low shrubs. The space was, Weyr saw, effectively concealed from the audience by the backdrop. "That's where the two of you should be when you're not onstage. If you want to check out the house, do it before we start. When the show is on, you should stay out of sight behind the backdrop. There's an old saying about that: 'If you can see the audience, they can see you.' And they shouldn't."

Kamlar and Weyr helped unpack the props and laid them out in the backstage area, and then helped Nomer put together a small table for the stage. A cluster of Tamish children watched them from inside the fence at the top of the hill. Occasionally an adult joined them. The short

Tamish man who was the manager shooed the onlookers away from time to time, but there always seemed to be a small cluster of the curious observing them. If traveling performers had come to Bown, Weyr supposed, he would have been among the onlookers. It seemed strange to be watched, rather than watching.

The number of onlookers increased in the early afternoon when Weyr and Kamlar rehearsed with Nomer and Relinda in order to get used to the new stage. As far as Weyr could tell, the rehearsal went well. He sang "River Wide, Boatman Ride" once with Nomer and Relinda, and he and Kamlar managed to remember most of the instructions Nomer had given them about the props. After the rehearsal they carefully lined up the props backstage. Weyr felt confident about his part in the magic performance.

But as the afternoon wore on and Weyr realized that the show would soon begin, he felt a tightness in his stomach. The manager bustled about, talking rapidly with Nomer or Relinda. Somehow the man's fussing made Weyr more nervous. Late in the afternoon Nomer laid out food, leftovers from the previous night. Weyr could eat little. Nomer and Relinda ate sparingly, too, Weyr noticed. And Kamlar ate nothing. Just after the meal, Weyr accidentally knocked over one of the props in the backstage area, a large metal plate. It clattered as it fell. Kamlar jumped at the sound.

"Opening-show jitters, boys?" Nomer said.

"What?" Weyr and Kamlar said together.

"This is your first time onstage, even if it's only a walk-on," Nomer said. "I daresay you might be a bit nervous."

"I'm not . . ." Weyr began, and stopped. His stomach

still felt tight. He smiled ruefully. "Maybe I am, a little."

"I am. More than a little," Kamlar said.

"Don't worry," Nomer said. "Even the most experienced of us get it some." He looked at Relinda, who was adjusting a strap on her lythe. "Butterflies under the ribs, Rel?"

"You're one to talk!" Relinda said.

Nomer chuckled.

A few minutes later, though there was still ample natural light, the manager lit the braziers in front of the stage. People began to enter the amphitheatre. Some brought blankets to sit on. A few had servants who carried wooden stools. They chattered in Tam. Weyr's nervousness increased as he peered at them from behind the stage backdrop. There appeared to be several hundred people on the hill. Light from the braziers blended with late-afternoon sunlight to glaze the faces of those nearest him.

The Instrument and most of his guards sat on the ground midway up the hill. Berthin was with them. She had announced earlier in the afternoon that she wanted to see Weyr perform from the audience. Valmo and another guard stood behind the stage, out of the way of Nomer, Relinda, Weyr, and Kamlar, but close enough to keep a watchful eye on them.

As Weyr looked at the crowd, for an instant he felt his hearing extend. He heard distinct voices speak in Tam amidst the general babble, two male voices, deep, and, he thought, a bit tense. One of them mentioned the Instrument's name.

"Close enough to show time that you should stay out of sight, Weyr," Nomer said behind him in a crisp voice.

"Right, Nomer," Weyr said, slightly embarrassed.

Weyr moved behind the backdrop. The sound of the Tamish voices was gone. Weyr wondered for a moment who the two men were and why they were talking about the Instrument. He shook his head. He had work to do. He could think about that later.

Nomer put an arm around Relinda's shoulder. "This close to Domn, I guess we're still a bit of a draw, even after more than two years, eh, Rel?" he said.

"That's something, at least," Relinda said.

Nomer and Relinda slipped into the bushes behind the backstage area for a few moments and emerged dressed in Tamish chiba. Nomer's robe was a solid deep blue, Relinda's silver flecked with gold. The cloth in both appeared to be expensive but worn. Nomer and Relinda looked, Weyr thought, like a particularly handsome Tamish couple dressed for some formal occasion. Weyr remembered what Relinda had said about Nomer's ability to pass for a Tam.

Relinda slung her lythe over her shoulder. A small stair led up to a slit in the backdrop through which one could enter the wagon stage. Nomer and Relinda stood together just below the stair. Relinda plucked softly at the lythe, adjusting the tuning. Kamlar came up beside Weyr.

"Kamlar, Weyr, may you have a thousand toothaches out there," Nomer said.

"Beg pardon?" Weyr said.

Nomer grinned. "That's an actor's way of wishing someone luck in a show, Weyr. It's a kind of a reverse curse."

"Oh," Weyr said. The tightness in his stomach lessened

a little. He grinned back at Nomer. "A thousand tooth-aches to you, too, then."

"Thanks, Weyr," Relinda said.

Weyr heard steps on the stage. The audience quieted.

"Ladies and gentlemen, brothers and sisters," the manager's voice said from the other side of the backdrop. "After their absence for two years on an extended and unprecedentedly successful tour in Carda and other points in the west, we are pleased to have with us again one of the great performing teams of our generation. Please welcome Nomer and Relinda!"

The applause was loud and boisterous. Nomer leaned toward Relinda and gave her a light kiss on the cheek.

"We're on," Nomer said. "Mind your cues, Weyr, Kamlar."

"We will," Weyr said.

Nomer followed Relinda up the stairway and through the slit in the curtain onto the stage. Weyr heard Relinda onstage strum a loud chord on the lythe. The audience noise subsided. For an instant Weyr half expected the odd wordless Agari melody of "The Call." Instead Nomer and Relinda began a lively Tamish drinking song. Weyr smiled wryly at himself. This audience was Tamish. Nomer and Relinda were, as far as the audience was concerned, Tamish performers. They would hardly begin with an Agari song. Weyr listened to Nomer and Relinda. The two voices, resonant bass and rich, low soprano, rang clear and strong. There was a slight echo back from the amphitheatre. The audience applauded as they heard the first few words of the song and again as the song ended.

The show had begun.

Chapter Fourteen

NOMER AND RELINDA slid easily into another lively song, then another. By the third song, the audience was clapping in rhythm to the music. A quiet Tam ballad brought silence. Weyr could hear no sound save a gentle rustle of wind in the scrub brushes behind him and Nomer and Relinda's intertwining voices. As the audience applauded the ballad, Weyr edged up the steps to the curtain at the back of the stage. "River Wide, Boatman Ride" would come next, Nomer had told him. Weyr's stomach turned over.

"A thousand toothaches, Weyr," Kamlar whispered.

"Thanks, Kam."

"Friends," Nomer's voice said from the other side of the backdrop, "we've asked a young performer of great promise to join us for our next song. He's making his first stage appearance. Please greet Weyr of Bown."

Weyr gulped as he came through the slit in the backdrop and onto the stage to the sound of polite applause. His throat felt dry and his knees seemed a little wobbly. The sight of several hundred strange faces all turned toward him was unnerving. When he had sung in Bown, there had never been more than forty or fifty people in the audience, and he had known all of them. This was different, very different. Nomer put an arm around Weyr's shoulders and led him to the front of the stage beside Relinda.

Relinda struck the opening chords of "River Wide, Boatman Ride," and Nomer lined out the bawdy words of the first verse. When Weyr joined in the chorus, his voice felt constricted and weak to him. For a moment, he wondered if he could sing at all. Nomer's big hand squeezed his shoulder gently in rhythm to the beat of the song. The touch was reassuring. Weyr heard Nomer's melody and Relinda's harmony clearly. In his mind he found the spaces between the notes where his voice should go. His throat relaxed. His voice sounded much fuller and more natural to him. The second time through the chorus, the singing came easily, the third more so. Weyr even added one or two notes of harmony he had never used in rehearsal and felt Nomer give his shoulder an extra little squeeze.

They finished the song on a sustained chord. Weyr was slightly surprised by the burst of applause that followed. During the latter part of the song, he had hardly been conscious of the presence of the audience at all. The tightness in his stomach and the constriction in his throat were completely gone. Weyr felt exhilarated. The audience had obviously enjoyed the song, and that was a good thing, but somehow the fact that the song had sounded right to him was more satisfying. Weyr bowed once with Relinda and Nomer and made his way backstage.

"That sounded good!" Kamlar whispered. Late-afternoon sunlight caught the Agari boy's blue eyes and gave them a glint. "You were wonderful! Were you nervous?"

"Yes," Weyr said. "But only at the beginning."

Nomer and Relinda sang several more songs and then launched into their magic performance. Weyr and Kamlar were kept busy organizing and supplying the props as Nomer had instructed them. Just before they came onstage with a prop for the first time, Weyr gave Kamlar the toothache curse. Kamlar grinned nervously. But as far as Weyr could tell, they managed the props without a mistake.

The sun had almost set when Nomer and Relinda concluded the magic performance with the trick box and the swords. Kamlar and Weyr carried the box offstage. A breeze had come up. With the breeze and the declining sun, Weyr felt chilly. He put on the jacket Relinda had given him. Kamlar, too, donned a jacket.

"Well, that's that," Weyr whispered to Kamlar. "How do you feel? Were you nervous?"

"Only at first, like you said," Kamlar said. "I feel terrific."

"Me, too."

They settled onto the ground behind the backdrop. Weyr felt relaxed and easy. Their role in the show was over. Nomer and Relinda were now going to do a scene from a play. That was the one part of the show he had not heard before. Idly he wished he could slip out in front of the stage to watch, or at least peek at Nomer and Relinda around the backdrop. But Nomer had been very firm about not being seen.

Weyr smiled to himself. There was a way he could see and hear the scene without making himself visible to the audience, if he could manage it. After all, he had watched Nomer and Relinda from the audience's point of view during a rehearsal of *The Peacemaker.* Somehow, the way he felt now, at once relaxed and concentrated, seemed very similar to the way he had felt then.

Weyr closed his eyes and tried to extend his sight. To his delight, the sense responded. Weyr imagined himself in a spot out on the hill in the audience. The stage came into his vision. Nomer and Relinda stood poised at opposite ends of the small platform. Nomer opened his mouth to speak.

But the voice Weyr heard was not Nomer's.

"The filthy Instrument's down there," the voice whispered. "It's dark enough. Let's do it now!"

"Yes! Now!" another voice whispered.

Weyr snapped alert. The second voice sounded familiar. It was one of the voices he had heard speak the Instrument's name before the beginning of the show. Weyr moved his sight so that he was looking not at the stage but into the audience. He saw four Tamish men rise from the rear of the amphitheatre. One pointed at the Instrument and his guards. The men moved slowly down among the clusters of people toward them.

"Cautiously, cautiously," one of the men whispered. "Remember the timing. Surprise is our best weapon."

What were the men doing? What did they want with the Instrument? He should warn the Instrument about the men, Weyr thought. But how could he? He couldn't interrupt Nomer and Relinda's performance. In any case, the

Instrument was protected by his guards. What could the men do? But the Instrument should know about them. They could be dangerous.

Weyr opened his eyes for a moment and glanced around him. Valmo. He could tell Valmo about the men. Valmo could warn the Instrument. Weyr lurched to his feet, took a few steps toward Valmo, and stopped. What could he say to him? How could he explain what he had seen and heard?

But he *had* to do something. For a moment Weyr stood rigid, his arms tight against his sides. He could not move.

"Weyr! What's wrong?" Kamlar whispered. The other boy came up beside him. "What are you doing?"

"Kam!" Weyr said, also in a whisper. "I heard some Tamish men out there in the audience talking about your father. They sounded threatening."

"You heard people in the audience?" Kamlar said. "How could you hear them from here?"

"I have . . . very sharp ears," Weyr said desperately. "I tell you, I heard them. They're going to do something to your father."

"Who? What could anybody do to him?" Kamlar said. "The guards are with him. Nobody would dare do something here. And anyway, how could you hear . . ."

"Filthy Agari! Filthy Agari witch!" a loud voice shouted.

Weyr closed his eyes again for a moment. The four men had moved down through the audience so that they stood a few yards above the Instrument and his guards.

"Why do you bring your cursed Agari witchcraft here to defile us, Nomer of Elubin?" the voice shouted.

Weyr opened his eyes again. With Kamlar close behind him, he ran to the edge of the backdrop and peered around it. The man who spoke was short and stocky for a Tam. His face was covered with a dark-brown beard. His arm was raised. One finger pointed toward the stage. Weyr's senses had returned to normal, but now he did not need the extended senses to hear or see the man.

"You play at magic, Nomer of Elubin, you and your traitorous Tam wife, but you practice witchcraft, like all Agari butchers," the man on the hill shouted. "The vengeance of the Tam will not be long in coming."

The audience, which had been silent, began to murmur. A few people half rose. Valmo strode up beside Weyr and Kamlar. Out of the corner of his eye Weyr saw the other guard move to the opposite end of the backdrop. Against the growing crowd noise Weyr heard Nomer and Relinda's voices. They were evidently trying to continue the performance despite the interruption.

"And there sits the Agari witch's master," the man on the hill shouted. His arm came down. His finger pointed at the Instrument. "A chief of the Agari butchers, the Agari Instrument. We remember Gliddon!"

The murmur in the audience grew into an excited, confused babble of voices. The man shouted more, but Weyr could no longer understand his words. Shapes rose from the hillside near the Instrument. The guards. Beside Weyr, Valmo drew his sword. He spun away from Weyr and Kamlar and began to push his way through the audience and up the hill toward the Instrument. Out of the corner of his eye, Weyr saw the guard from the other side of the backdrop do the same.

"My father!" Kamlar said. "They're going to do something to my father. I've got to help him!"

Kamlar took a few steps away from the backdrop. Weyr turned to see a shadowy figure jump at Kamlar and grab him around the waist from the back. Another figure was close on the heels of the first. He threw a cloth bag over Kamlar's head. Kamlar screamed, but the sound was lost in the noise of the crowd.

Weyr leaped toward Kamlar. Strong arms gripped him from behind and stopped him in his tracks. Weyr clutched at the arms. He tried to kick backward. The grip tightened. Weyr opened his mouth to yell. Coarse cloth scraped his face and cut off his vision. A bag had been slipped over his head, too. A hand jammed cloth into his mouth. Something pressed against his throat. Weyr could make no sound.

"We've got the boy," a male voice said from a short distance away.

"And we've got another one," a harsh male voice close to Weyr's ear said.

"Which one is the Instrument's brat?" the first voice said. "They both look like filthy Agari."

"No matter," a female voice said. "There's no time. Take them both. Faran can't distract Lakren's guards for long."

Weyr's stomach churned as he was lifted into the air. He jostled against a hard body and knew his captor was running.

"Through the bushes there!" the same female voice said. Her voice had a staccato rhythm. "Terif will have the horses."

Weyr felt thorny branches scrape against his hands. He heard a horse whinny. The coarse cloth still clogged his mouth. He could hardly breathe. Weyr spat the cloth out and tried to shout. He kicked out wildly with his legs and felt one foot connect with bone. A voice near his ear cursed in Tam.

"This one's fighting like a mountain cat," the harsh voice near his ear said.

"Put him out. Put them both out," the female voice said. "But not too roughly. The Instrument's whelp is useless to us dead."

Weyr felt something hard strike the base of his skull. He thought he heard Kamlar's muffled voice before he blacked out.

Chapter Fifteen

WEYR WOKE IN a sitting position, with the feel of hard rock against his back and the smell of damp earth in his nostrils. His stomach ached. The base of his head hurt. He tried to reach a hand up to touch his head and could not. Weyr twisted his wrists and felt something cut into them. His hands were tied behind his back. He tried to shift his legs, but they would not move, either. Weyr looked at them. They were bound together with thick rope.

Weyr's eyes adjusted to dim light. He looked upward. The light was moonlight, he realized. Perhaps twenty feet above him he saw an irregular domed ceiling. A jagged circular hole in the center of the ceiling admitted light. One of the moons — Weyr thought it was Danger — shone through the hole. Rock walls sloped down from the ceiling. Weyr was leaning against one of them. A rough wooden door was set into the wall to his right. Next to it were a few crude wooden shelves. Slivers of light filtered in around the edges of the door onto a dirt floor. Except for the door and the shelves, the formation of the room was natural, not human-made. He was in a cave.

Weyr heard something stir a few feet away from him. In the dim light he could see a human form propped up against the wall of the cave opposite him. It was Kamlar. His arms and legs seemed to be bound, too.

"Kam," Weyr said. "Kam! Are you awake?"

"Um. What?" Kamlar's voice sounded drowsy for a moment, then came alert. "Weyr, is that you?"

"It's me."

"Where are we?"

"We're in some kind of cave."

"A cave?"

"Yes."

"A cave." Kamlar shook his head. He frowned. "Then we must be somewhere up in the Hills," he said. "The Hills of Karmon are full of caves." Kamlar shifted his weight and tried to move. "I'm tied up. Somebody's tied me up. How did we get here?"

"I don't know," Weyr said. "I'm tied up, too. I don't remember anything after we were attacked."

"I remember somebody out in the audience shouting about my father and . . . Faran!"

"What?"

"Faran. The man who was shouting. His name is Faran. I couldn't see him too clearly in the crowd. But I know his voice."

"Who is Faran?"

"He's . . . ow!"

"What's wrong?"

"Ab splatter! My head hurts when I move it."

"Mine, too. They must have hit us hard. I didn't wake up until just a minute ago. Did you?"

"No."

"My stomach hurts, too," Weyr said.

"So does mine," Kamlar said. "I remember now. I heard horses just before I passed out. They must have tied us to horses. Like sacks. Where was Valmo? Where was the other guard who was backstage with us?"

"They went up the hill to protect your father."

Kamlar was silent for a moment.

"Clever," Kamlar said. "Very clever. Faran must have distracted my father's guards so the others could get us. I hope they caught him."

"Why would they want to get us?"

"I can guess. Not us, really. Me. It's me they wanted, I'm sure. In the shadows backstage I imagine we looked alike. You look almost Agari in that jacket. They probably couldn't tell which one was me."

"Why would they want you?"

"Probably to hold for ransom. To try to get my father to do something," Kamlar said. "Look, Weyr, can you move over here? Maybe if we get closer together, we can untie each other."

Weyr tried to stand and could not. Awkwardly he felt behind his back. The rope around his hands was attached to a heavy wooden pole stuck into the floor of the cave. He tugged at his bonds. The rope chafed at his wrists. The pole would not move.

"I'm tied down," Weyr said. "I can't move."

"Me, too," Kamlar said after a minute. "I'm roped to some kind of pole. Whoever tied us knew what they were doing." Kamlar frowned again. "They knew what they were doing when they took us, too. They couldn't have had much time. They must have had it all planned out, where we'd be, how they could grab us."

"How would they know we were there?"

Kamlar cocked his head and paused, thinking. His face looked pale in the moonlight.

"It wouldn't have been too hard to find out that my father's party would be in Warn," Kamlar said. "They could have watched us while we traveled. Or someone could have sold them that information."

"Sold them the information?" Weyr said.

"People buy information, Weyr. Even my father buys information sometimes. So somehow, they probably knew we were going to be in Warn. Then they could have watched us when we set up for the show. There were a lot of people around."

"I remember."

"They could have figured out where we'd be during the show," Kamlar said. "It was just getting dark, wasn't it? Perfect timing. Did you see any of the ones who caught us?"

"Not really. It was too dark. I heard two men's voices and a woman's voice. That's all."

"The woman might be Jocarra. She and Faran were part of the same group."

"Who is this Faran?" Weyr asked.

"Faran is — was — one of the leaders of a group in Domn called the Alliance."

"Who are they?"

"It's a long story, and I only know part of it. My father's

told me some. I'm supposed to keep myself informed about politics in Domn. That's part of my 'Tamish education,'" Kamlar said. His voice was slightly sarcastic.

"What about politics in Domn? What's this Alliance?"

"The Alliance is a group of Tam who don't like what they call 'Agari influence' in Domn. That means people like my father. They hate us," Kamlar said. "That isn't what they say. They say they're for preserving the old Tamish ways and customs. But what it boils down to is that they hate the Agari and want them out of Domn."

"What do they do, the Alliance?"

"For a while they mostly just talked. Stuff about how the 'Agari influence' was corrupting Tamish ways. They talked a lot about the glories of ancient Tam, the great old kings and warriors and things, too. They had meetings and gave plays and made speeches in the streets and so on. That's where I heard Faran — from a distance, but I'd recognize that voice anywhere. He was one of their street orators. Then, about three or four years ago, they started to harass the Agari. They beat some people up. There were some burnings of Agari buildings, and a couple of people got killed."

"The Alliance did that?"

"They claimed they hadn't done it, that it was Tam fanatics. Still, people thought the Alliance was partly responsible. At least my father did. But the Alliance had some friends among The Twelve, so nothing happened to them."

Weyr's head throbbed. He found Kamlar's story bewildering. Occasionally he had heard stories from travelers at Anzia's Inn about burnings and other trouble in Carda.

But no one had suggested they had anything to do with the Agari. Certainly nothing like what Kamlar was describing had ever happened in Bown.

"What's 'The Twelve'?" Weyr said.

"The Twelve are the big, important Tam families in Domn. Actually there are only seven families now, but a long time ago there used to be twelve, so people still call them The Twelve. They pretty well control Domn, when they agree on something, which they don't always."

"And they don't like the Agari, either?"

"Some of them are anti-Agari, my father says, though they don't admit it in public. Others aren't. But the ones who are sometimes give Agaris, particularly the merchants my father represents, a hard time."

"And this Faran — he's one of them?"

"You mean one of the families of The Twelve?"

"Yes."

"No. I don't know a lot about him, except that he was one of the leaders of the Alliance. He's not from Domn originally, I think. I believe he's a Mountain Tam. From up in the Hills."

"What about the woman you mentioned, the one you said I might have heard talking? What's her name?"

"Jocarra. Now she *is* from one of the families of The Twelve, the Beman. In public the Beman disowned her after Gliddon, but some people think her family is still secretly in touch with her."

"Gliddon," Weyr said. "I remember now. That man shouting on the hill — Faran — said 'We remember Gliddon.' What's 'Gliddon'?"

"Gliddon is a section of Domn. It's what they call a

mixed area. Most parts of the city are mainly Tam, and a few are mainly Agari. Gliddon is both, and there's a lot of tension there between Tam and Agari. Or so they say. I've never been in Gliddon. My father won't let me go there. It's a rough area. A couple of years ago, when the anti-Agari feelings were strongest, there was a riot in Gliddon."

"A what?"

"A riot. Bunches of Tam went out raiding and burning Agari houses and shops, especially in the poorest part of Gliddon. It spilled over into some of the all-Agari areas. Some Agari went raiding back in Tam areas. It went on for quite a few days. Several people were killed, and a lot were hurt. There was talk that the Alliance had started it."

"Did they?"

"Maybe. Nobody knows for sure how it started, I think. Some of the Alliance leaders — particularly Faran and Jocarra — were in the thick of it, urging people on, that's for sure. Like I said, it lasted for quite a while. I remember I couldn't go out of my father's house for days. His guards were all over the place."

"That sounds like something."

"It was. After a while The Twelve finally agreed to work together. They lent their private guards to the City Guard and finally stopped the rioting. Things have settled down since then, but there was a lot of hard feeling in the city. Some people had to leave, like Nomer and Relinda."

"Nomer and Relinda were involved in the riot at Gliddon?" Weyr said, surprised. "I remember Relinda told me they had to leave Domn because of some political trouble, but she didn't say what it was. What did they do?"

"My father says they were trying to calm things down.

They had — still have, I guess — a lot of prestige in Domn because they were so well known as actors. But people on both sides blamed them. My cousin Romely said that's because he's Agari and she's Tam. So they had to leave."

"Nomer and Relinda are going back to Domn now, though," Weyr said.

"Right. Things have settled down some. That's why my father was able to convince them to come back from Carda."

"What happened to this Faran and Jocarra?"

"After Gliddon they left Domn, too. There hasn't been too much talk about them since then as far as I know, but there were rumors that they were living in the Hills of Karmon, like bandits. Nobody knew for sure."

"If you're right about who brought us here, Kam, we know," Weyr said. "We know for sure where they are."

"If we knew where *we* are," Kamlar said with a snort. "Like I said, the Hills of Karmon are honeycombed with caves. We could be anywhere."

Weyr moved slightly. The ropes tugged at his wrists.

"What will they do to us — this Faran and Jocarra, if it is them?" Weyr said.

"I don't know. They're fanatics. They hate the Agari." Kamlar paused. "And they hate Tam who associate with Agari — 'tame Tam,' they call them — even more."

It was not cold in the cave, but Weyr shivered. They sat in silence for a moment. A brown salam scurried across the dirt floor of the cave. Weyr heard a wolf howl in the distance.

"Kam, are you scared?" Weyr said.

Kamlar shifted his weight against the wall on his side of the cave. His face was very pale in the dim light.

"Yes, Weyr, I'm scared," Kamlar said. "I'm very scared."

"Me, too," Weyr said.

~

He and Kamlar talked for a time longer, but Weyr did not learn much more. In a way Weyr could not quite understand, Kamlar thought he had somehow betrayed his father by allowing himself to be captured. Kamlar also worried out loud about what the kidnappers would do with Weyr. They might, he thought, be easy on him because he was Tam, or they might hate him because he had been found in the company of Agari. After a time, Kamlar closed his eyes. Weyr watched him as he drifted off to sleep, troubled by a thought he could not share with Kamlar.

Weyr was sure that he was at least partly responsible for their capture.

He had stood by, paralyzed, while the kidnappers had carried out their plan. Weyr was not sure it would have made any difference if he had sounded an alarm before the men began to make their move. The whole thing had happened very fast. But the fact was, he had known there was danger and had done nothing. If Kamlar felt as though he had betrayed his father, Weyr felt as though he had betrayed Kamlar. The guilty thought weighed on Weyr until finally, his head still a dull ache, he fell into an exhausted and troubled sleep.

Chapter Sixteen

WEYR CAME AWAKE to the sound of shuffling outside the wooden door in the wall next to him.
Sunlight glinted through cracks along the sides of the
door. He glanced at Kamlar and saw that he was just
opening his eyes.

The door opened. A stocky man of perhaps forty entered the cave carrying a metal kettle. He was dressed in
an ordinary brown Tamish tob and blav, but he had a
bright-red bandana tied across his forehead. His face was
brown, flat, and broad in the Tamish way, though his nose
was crooked, as though it had been broken and never
healed properly. The man had a knife sheathed on one side
of his belt. Weyr struggled to rise, felt the ropes tug at
him, and fell back.

"Who are you?" Kamlar said. His treble voice was loud
and strident. It echoed slightly in the small cave. "Why did
you do this to us? I am Kamlar, the son of the Instrument
of the Merchants of Elubin. My father will see to it
that . . ."

"I know perfectly well who you are. Save the bluster for the Agari lackeys who might listen to it, lad," the man said. His voice sounded more amused than angry. He moved to the wooden shelf near the door and took down two thin metal plates and two metal spoons. "Or tell it to Jocarra, if you think that'll help. I'm just your jailer."

"So I was right," Kamlar said. He glanced at Weyr and nodded slightly. "Jocarra *is* here."

"You'd already figured that out, eh, lad?" the man said. His voice was nasal. He ladled food from the kettle onto the two plates. "I suppose you recognized Faran and decided if it was one of them, it was probably both of them. You're a smart one. They said that about you in Domn."

"What do you want?" Kamlar said.

"I'm not the one to say. Like I told you, I'm just your jailer. My name's Terif. Jocarra will be along in a while. She's got something she wants you to do." Terif scratched his crooked nose and picked up a plate. "Right now I've brought you breakfast."

"I'm not hungry," Kamlar said. His voice was sullen.

"That's certainly a lie," Terif said. "I've never seen a lad your age who wasn't hungry most of the time. We're not barbarians, whatever lies your Agari mouthpieces tell about us. We'll feed you. And you'll eat. You're no good to us starved to death."

Terif gave a nasal chortle, set the plate in front of Kamlar, and moved behind him.

"I'm going to untie your hands so you can feed yourself. I don't relish serving you like a baby," Terif said. "But don't get any ideas about being a hero by coming at me. In the first place, I'm a lot bigger than you are. In the second place, I'm not going to untie your legs. And finally, even if you got away, we're in the middle of the Hills of Karmon. You'd be lost outside in ten minutes and end up food for a hungry wolf pack or frozen to death at night."

When his bonds were loosened, Kamlar tensed his shoulders. For an instant Weyr thought Kamlar was going to try to attack Terif, despite the man's warning, but after a moment Kamlar relaxed and began to eat. Watching him eat made Weyr hungry, too. He remembered that neither of them had eaten much the night before.

"I don't know where you fit," Terif said as he placed the other plate in front of Weyr and began to loosen the rope around his wrists. "You're a Tam if I ever saw a Tam, though it was hard to tell that yesterday. Maybe you're an accident. Or maybe you're one of the Instrument's tame Tam. Jocarra will decide what to do with you."

Weyr rubbed his wrists where the rope had chafed them and looked at the food. It was a version of three-bean wurd, he saw. Weyr swallowed a spoonful. It tasted bland and flavorless.

"Don't bind them again yet, Terif," said a woman's voice. "Our Agari, at least, has to do a little writing first."

Weyr looked up. A thin, almost emaciated, young woman stood silhouetted against the sunlight in the doorway, her hands on her slim waist. Her face was narrow for a Tam, her skin a few shades lighter than Terif's. Her black hair was tied back with a red bandana similar to the one Terif wore. Like Terif, she had a knife sheathed at her belt. In her hand she carried a ragged sheet of paper and a blunt piece of charcoal. She walked across the cave and stood in front of Kamlar. Her step was light, nervous.

"The boy already knew you were here, Jocarra," Terif said.

"I imagined he would," Jocarra said.

"Why have you done this?" Kamlar said. "How do you dare to . . ."

"Please do not waste my time with boyish bravado," Jocarra said. Her voice had a thin, brittle edge to it. She clipped her words out in a staccato volley. "In Domn you had a reputation for being intelligent, whenever anyone saw you off your father's leash. Act your reputation. You know who we are and what we represent."

"I know," Kamlar said.

"If you are as intelligent as everyone says, you also presumably have realized by now why you're here," Jocarra said. "We have no intention of harming you, at least for the moment. We do not stoop to dealing with children, except when we must as part of our plan. Our business is with your father. There are certain things we want to . . . ask . . . of him."

"What things?" Kamlar said.

"There is no reason for you to know that. What we need now is for you to write to your father. We'll send what you write along with certain . . . requests . . . we want to make of him. Knowing you're alive and with us will no doubt make him more willing to negotiate."

"You're going to blackmail him," Kamlar said. "You're going to ask for a ransom."

"Say rather that we are going to ask for certain political concessions, among them money," Jocarra said.

She dropped the ragged paper onto the dirt floor in front of Kamlar and drew her knife. Weyr gasped, afraid the woman would use the knife on Kamlar, but she merely whittled the charcoal she held to a crude point with a few strokes of the blade. The woman was left-handed, Weyr noticed. Jocarra crouched down in front of Kamlar and held the charcoal out to him.

"A short note will do, in either Tam or Agari. I read both," Jocarra said. "Just 'I'm alive and a prisoner' or some such, written in your own hand. I'm sure your father will recognize the writing."

"What if I won't?" Kamlar said. He lifted his chin defiantly, but his voice did not seem altogether steady.

"Please don't be tedious," Jocarra said. "There are many things we can do if you won't. Faran, who is, I suppose you know, part of our organization, has any number of unpleasant persuasive skills, if it comes to that. He'll be here tonight."

"So!" Terif said. "He got away."

"I saw his signal just before I came down here," Jocarra said. She glanced at Terif. "The fire in the Agari camp must have worked perfectly as a secondary diversion. He's on his way here, but I doubt that he'll come before nightfall. He'll have to move cautiously. I imagine Lakren's people are swarming the Hills."

"Much good it will do them. Or these two, here," Terif said. He laughed mirthlessly.

"I don't think we'll need to wait for Faran, though," Jocarra said. She turned back to Kamlar and waved the charcoal under his nose. "Surely your father will want to know that you're alive. He must be worried to distraction about his only son and the heir to all the Agari pretensions in Domn. That should be reason enough for you to write to reassure him. I'm not telling you to write to ask him for anything. We'll do that. I simply want you to prove to him that you're alive and with us."

Kamlar frowned. His breath came in a low hiss between his teeth.

"All right, I'll write it," Kamlar said. He took the charcoal from Jocarra and eyed it dubiously.

"Very sensible," Jocarra said. Her lip curled up. She said sarcastically, "I'm sorry that we don't have the more elegant writing materials to which you're no doubt accustomed. In the mountains one must make do with what one has."

Kamlar frowned, then bent over the sheet of paper on the floor and began to write. Jocarra straightened up and turned to face Weyr.

"Now for you," Jocarra said to Weyr. "We hadn't bargained on two, but both of you were dressed alike and we were in a hurry. In the shadows it was impossible to tell you weren't Agari. Even after we discovered you were Tam, it seemed prudent to keep you. Who are you?"

"My name is Weyr."

"Well, Weyr, why were you with the Instrument's party, with the two actors?"

"He isn't part of anything," Kamlar said. He looked up from his writing. "He doesn't know a thing about any of this — Domn, or the Alliance, or any of it. He's never even been in Domn. His family's dead. He was traveling alone to Domn to meet a cousin there. We invited him to ride with us."

"You finish your writing," Jocarra said with a glance at

Kamlar. She turned back to Weyr. Her brown eyes looked hard. "Is what he says true?"

"It's true," Weyr said.

"What's your cousin's name?"

No one had ever asked Weyr that question. He fumbled for an answer.

"Borno," Weyr said, taking the first name that came into his mind. "His name is Borno."

"Which Borno? Borno's one of the most common Tam names there are. I know twenty Bornos in Domn. Borno the shoemaker? Lame Borno? Borno, Jolar's son?" Jocarra said.

"Just Borno."

"And where in Domn were you to go to meet this cousin of yours named Borno?" Jocarra asked. She arched an eyebrow skeptically.

"He lives in Gliddon," Weyr said. It was the only place name he knew in Domn. "Just before she died, my Gran told me to look for him in Gliddon."

"Where in Gliddon? What street? What place?"

"I . . . I don't remember," Weyr said.

"You're lying," Jocarra said.

"It doesn't matter," Kamlar said. He had finished writing. He held the ragged sheet of paper in one hand. The hand was not altogether steady. "What I told you is true. He doesn't have anything to do with Domn, or my father, or politics. He's from out near Carda. He just happened to be with us. You should let him go. He's one of you. He's Tam."

"Unfortunately, not all Tam are with us," Jocarra said.

"People like your father have seen to that. This one does seem a bit young to be a thoroughly tame Tam, though. There may still be hope for him. It's possible we may let him go."

Weyr's mouth was dry. He tried to lick his lips. They were dry, too. It was hard to swallow.

"I don't want you to let me go," Weyr said. "I don't want you to let me go unless you let Kamlar go, too. I'll stay with him. He's my friend."

"A noble boyish sentiment, that," Jocarra said. Her lip turned up slightly. "If we do let you go, I can assure you it won't be out of sentimentality because you're Tam." She took the letter from Kamlar and read it quickly. "This seems adequate," she said. She turned back to Weyr. "But if what your Agari *friend*" — Jocarra made the word sound derisive — "has just written here doesn't bring the Instrument to terms, perhaps we'll free you in a place where you can take a message to Lakren."

"What message?" Weyr said.

"Faran tells me ears can be lopped off rather easily and without too much mess," Jocarra said. "They're not heavy to carry, either. If you took an Agari ear back to Lakren, it might make a convincing message."

Weyr glanced at Kamlar. The Agari boy chewed at his lower lip. His face was pale. Weyr's stomach churned. For a moment he thought he might throw up. He swallowed hard. His saliva tasted bitter.

"Tie them again, Terif," Jocarra said.

Terif bound Kamlar and then Weyr. Neither of them tried to do anything to stop him. He then joined Jocarra at the door.

"Lest you get any boyish ideas about heroic measures of escape," Jocarra said, "you might know that Terif once worked the big boats on Lake Gor. He is an expert on knots. And he will be waiting just outside."

Jocarra and Terif left. After the heavy door slammed shut behind them, Weyr heard wood chunk against stone. Light again seeped between the edges of the door and the door frame. There was a break in the light at waist height. Weyr thought his senses might have extended for a moment. Whether they had or not, Weyr knew that a heavy wooden bar had been dropped across the door from the outside.

Chapter Seventeen

T HANK YOU, WEYR," Kamlar said. His voice was hoarse. He cleared his throat. "Thanks for saying you'd stay with me."

"I meant it," Weyr said.

"I know you did," Kamlar said. "But if they do decide to let you go, you should go."

"And leave you here? Jocarra said they'd let me go only if they . . ." Weyr could not complete the sentence.

"I heard her," Kamlar said. His voice wavered. Kamlar was trying not to cry, Weyr thought. Weyr was close to tears himself. "But at least then you'd be safe. They really only want me."

"I won't go!"

"You . . . you probably won't have any choice, anyway," Kamlar said. His voice was a little steadier. "They can make you go back to my father. Or at least they can take you somewhere else. If you get out, maybe you could lead my father back here."

"What chance is there of that?" Weyr said. "You told me yourself there are hundreds of caves up here in the Hills of

Karmon. And they'd never let me see where we are, even if I could remember."

"I know," Kamlar said. He frowned. "My father must be frantic. I'm sure he's got his guards and whoever else he could hire out looking for us."

"Can they find us?"

"Only if they're terribly lucky. Or if my father can buy information about Jocarra and her bunch from someone, which I doubt. Otherwise, every hill up here looks like every other hill."

"It wouldn't do us any good even if we could get out of here," Weyr said. "Terif said we'd freeze at night."

"I think he told us that mostly to scare us. I camped out up here in the summer with my father. It's cold in the Hills at night, but it's not that cold," Kamlar said. He paused. "We had tents, though."

"We can't get away anyhow," Weyr said.

"That's true," Kamlar said. He shifted against the wall on his side of the cave. "It'll be worse when Faran gets here. Terif doesn't seem really mean. He sounds, oh, like my father says, as though he thinks he's just doing a job. Even Jocarra sounded like she wouldn't do anything to us if she didn't believe she had to. But Faran's something else. I remember something my father told me once about Jocarra and Faran. He said 'While Jocarra is a fanatic, she's not bloodthirsty. But there's something animal about Faran.'"

Weyr swallowed hard. His saliva tasted bitter again.

"I'm responsible for us being here, you know," Weyr said.

"You're responsible? How can you be responsible?"

"I just am."

"That's ridiculous. Nobody's responsible for us being here except Jocarra and her bunch. What could you have done?"

"Nothing," Weyr said.

~

And yet the sense that he was somehow responsible for their kidnapping hung in Weyr's mind through the rest of the day. He said no more about it to Kamlar. But that did not keep him from thinking about it. His extended senses had given him a warning, but he had not acted on the warning. The memory of it was like a weight on Weyr's spirit. As the day passed, Weyr became more and more morose. He responded to Kamlar's attempts at talk only with monosyllables. At last he stopped talking altogether.

Twice more during the day — once at what seemed midday, and once when the light from the hole in the ceiling was growing dimmer — Terif came into the cave with a kettle to feed them. Each time, he took metal plates from the shelf near the door and ladled the same three-bean wurd they had eaten that morning onto their plates.

The first time Terif left, Weyr heard the wooden bar chunk into place outside the door. The second time he not only heard it. For a moment he could see the bar as well. Moreover, he could hear Jocarra's voice outside the cave, hear it not with his ears, but in his mind.

"Come up to the other cave, Terif," Jocarra said. Her brittle voice had a tone of authority. "I want you to be there when Faran comes. He should be here soon, and he's likely to be in one of his rages. He usually is after something big. You can handle him better than I can when he's in a rage."

"What about those two in the cave?" Terif said.

"What can they do? They're tied. You're the expert on that. The door is barred. I'm not worried about them getting out. I'm worried about what Faran may want to do to them, particularly the Instrument's brat, if he can get in at them."

"Where are the others?" Terif said.

"They're all up at the other cave already," Jocarra said. "Maybe if we . . ."

The voices faded. Weyr cursed under his breath. If only he could hear more of what Jocarra and the others would say, of what would happen when Faran came. Perhaps then he could think of something to do. Or if he could see outside the cave, that might help, too.

Fiercely, Weyr tried to send his senses to the spot outside the cave where he had heard Terif and Jocarra and seen the bar across the door. He tried to picture the bar in his mind, to will it into his sight. Nothing happened. Weyr cursed again. He had to try harder. A bead of sweat trickled down his temple as he tried to force an image of the bar into his mind. Still there was nothing.

No. That was not the right way. Willing the senses would not bring them under his control. He had discovered that before. But what was the right way? He had told himself he would wait until it came. Now there was no time to wait. He had to make the senses work. He had done it when he had watched the recognition scene from *The Peacemaker* and again during Nomer and Relinda's performance. How had he done it?

He had felt relaxed then, easy. But at the same time he had been full of the concentration that came with performance. Relax *and* concentrate. That was the key. He had to do both now.

He knew how to relax. Weyr said his meditation word to himself several times and began consciously to release each muscle in his body. He felt tension drain from his arms. The muscles in his legs went limp. But Weyr did not let his mind drift. Instead he kept his thoughts gently focused on the door to the cave. Relax, but concentrate on the door. Relax, but concentrate. Relax, but . . .

Slowly a picture of the bar across the door outside the cave formed in his mind. Weyr could see it clearly. Three or four inches thick, a few inches longer than the door was wide, the bar fitted into crevices in the rock on either side of the opening.

Weyr's mind was clear and relaxed, as it was when he meditated. But this sensation had none of the aimless quality of meditation. He was aware of where he was, of Kamlar's breathing across the cave, of his own cramped and aching body. Startled, Weyr realized that he had not closed his eyes, as he usually did when the extended sight came. With his eyes he saw Kamlar slumped against the wall opposite him. But at the same time in his mind he could also see the bar across the door outside. It was as though he had two sets of eyes, one his real eyes, and the other an inner pair of eyes in his head.

Weyr moved his inner vision away from the wooden bar to the inside of the cave and toward Kamlar. The two visions of Kamlar, one from his mind, and one from his eyes, merged briefly. He moved his extended sight again and looked at Kamlar from the back. At the same time he still saw Kamlar from the front with his eyes. Both visions held steady. The double view should be confusing, Weyr thought, but it was not. Each vision had its own clarity, separate and distinct.

"I can do it!" Weyr said.

"Um?" Kamlar said. "What did you say?"

"I can do it," Weyr said. "I can see you."

"You can what?"

"I can see you!" Weyr said.

"What are you talking about, Weyr?" Kamlar said. "You've hardly opened your mouth for an age and now all of a sudden you say you can see me. Of course you can see me. And I can see you. Not that the light is all that good. It must be getting dark outside. But I can see you, too. So what?"

"No, no, Kam," Weyr said. "I can see you and I can see around you. I can look behind you." Weyr moved his inner eyes down to Kamlar's wrists. "I can look at the ropes where Terif tied your hands together."

"You can look at the *ropes*?"

"Yes. I can see them where they're wrapped around your wrists."

"How can you? They're behind me. What in the name of The Powers are you talking about?"

Weyr took a deep breath.

"Listen, Kam," Weyr said. "Sometimes I can see things other people can't. It's hard to explain. It's like . . . like I can see around corners. And I can do it now. Your hands and the way Terif tied them together are as clear to me as if I was sitting right behind you."

"Are you serious?"

"Yes. I can see how the ropes are attached to the pole next to you, too. You don't believe me?"

"I don't know."

"Hold out some fingers, one, two, three, whatever, it doesn't matter," Weyr said. "Keep your hands behind your back so they don't show."

"I can't do anything else. All right, I'm holding out some fingers."

With his inner eyes Weyr focused on Kamlar's stubby fingers below his bound wrists.

"It's your right hand," Weyr said. "You're holding out three fingers on your right hand. Do it again with different fingers."

Kamlar grunted in astonishment. "I'm doing it," he said.

"Your left hand this time. Two fingers, thumb and pointer finger. Now do you believe me?"

"I believe you," Kamlar said. His voice was low, awed. "How do you do that?"

"I don't know. That doesn't matter right now. I just can do it. Move over beside the pole your hands are tied to. I'll tell you which parts of the rope to pull to untie the knots."

~

Kamlar was slow at first. Working behind his back was obviously not easy. He tugged awkwardly at the rope as Weyr told him what to do. Gradually Weyr learned to be more precise about his instructions. Kamlar's fingers moved more and more deftly at the knots. One knot came loose. Then another. At last Weyr saw the rope slip away from the pole behind Kamlar.

"I'm free! The rope is off the pole!" Kamlar said.

"I know," Weyr said. "I'm watching you, remember? Now come over and untie my hands. Then I can get you all the way loose."

Kamlar hobbled toward Weyr, his feet still roped together and his hands still tied behind his back.

"What if Terif comes back in?" Kamlar said. "Isn't he outside guarding us?"

"He's up in some different cave at a meeting with Jocarra and the others. They're waiting for Faran. They're a ways off. I heard them talking about it."

"You can *hear* like that, too?"

"Sometimes. Not now. But I think they're still up at the other cave. I don't know when they'll come back, though. Hurry!"

Kamlar sat down behind Weyr so they were back to back. His fingers grasped the rope around Weyr's wrists. Weyr watched him with his inner eyes and gave him instructions. Weyr could clearly see each twist of the rope, how the strands were bound together behind his back to form knots. It was an odd sensation, looking at himself from behind. Kamlar slowly loosened one strand after another. Once Weyr's extended vision faded. Weyr fought back panic. He began to chant his word again, forcing himself to relax. The vision returned.

"There! It's done!" Kamlar said at last. "You're free."

Weyr pulled his hands around in front of him and rubbed at the spots where he had been tied. It was now almost totally dark in the cave, but his vision with his inner eyes was still clear. As quickly as he could, Weyr untied the bonds around Kamlar's wrists and then the ropes around both their legs.

"Now let's get out of here," Weyr said.

"How do we do that?"

"There's a wooden bar across the door on the outside that keeps the door shut. I saw it."

"What good does that do?"

"There's enough space on either side of the door, between it and the frame, to get something between and under the bar so we can push the bar up."

"Like what?"

Weyr rapidly scanned the cave. His inner eyes lit on the metal plates on the shelf near the door.

"The plates!" Weyr said. "They're thin enough to fit in the spaces next to the door. We can push the bar up with the plates. You take one on one side and I'll take one on the other."

"Where are the plates? I can't see them. It's too dark."

"It's not dark for me," Weyr said. "I'll guide you."

Weyr snatched two plates from the shelf. He gripped Kamlar's elbow and led him to one side of the door, slipped one of the plates into the crack between the door and the frame and slid it up until he felt it touch the bottom of the bar.

"Grab this," Weyr said. He guided Kamlar's hand to the plate. "Don't push up until I say so. I'll get on the other side."

"Right."

Weyr shoved a second plate up against the bar on the opposite side of the door.

"All right, Kam," Weyr said. "Now! Push up hard!"

Weyr felt the muscles in his arms tense as he lifted his plate. He heard Kamlar grunt. With his inner eyes Weyr saw the other boy straining upward. Weyr felt the bar give slightly. Wood scraped on stone. Abruptly the weight of the bar was gone. The bar landed with a thud on the ground outside. Weyr pushed the door open.

"We're out," Weyr said.

The night was cloudy. With his eyes, Weyr could see neither stars nor moon. Kamlar was only a dim outline.

"Sweet Breath of Life!" Kamlar said. "What are you, Weyr? What in the Seven Levels of Torment are you? I've . . . I've heard about people who can do strange things. My father talks about that sometimes. And there are Agari tales about people who can look in places no one else can. Some folks say such people are witches." Kamlar paused. His voice lowered almost to a whisper. "Weyr, are you a witch?"

Weyr flinched at the word, but he could hear none of the fear that had been in the voices of the people in Bown. In Kamlar's voice there was only wonder.

"I don't know what I am," Weyr said. "I can just do those things, is all. Sometimes. Up to tonight, though, I couldn't do them when I wanted to. It just came and went. Does it matter what I am? We're out. We're free. We've got to get away."

"I can barely see anything," Kamlar said. "Where can we go? How can we go?"

"Grab the back of my shoulders and follow me," Weyr said. "I can see. I can see everything."

Chapter Eighteen

"WHERE ARE WE going?" Kamlar said.

"I don't know," Weyr said. "Anywhere away from here. Look! I think there's a trail over there."

"I can't see it. I can just barely make out the back of your head."

"Hold tight to my shoulders."

"I will."

As they started along the trail, Weyr heard a wolf howl. A cold gust of air caught his face. He pulled up the collar of his jacket.

The trail was a thin opening between low trees and bushes so close together that their branches caught on Weyr's jacket and scratched his arms as they walked. At first it sloped gently upward, twisting and turning around larger trees and big rocks. After a few minutes, the slope became steeper and more rocky. There were fewer bushes. Climbing became harder. They had to pause from time to time to catch their breath.

Weyr had no trouble leading the way. He saw the trail

as clearly as if it were daylight. He saw it more clearly, in fact, since he could look around a rock or a tree and sometimes pick an easier way. Walking with Kamlar holding on to his shoulders behind him was awkward at first. Kamlar occasionally stepped on Weyr's heels or stumbled on a rock. Eventually they developed a regular rhythm that let them move at a steady pace.

After they had walked for what Weyr guessed might have been an hour, the trail opened onto a broad, flat, stony ridge. A few scrubby plants, most of them no more than knee high, were the only vegetation. It was possible to walk side by side, with Weyr's arm around Kamlar's shoulder to guide him. The going was faster that way. The night air grew colder. A gusty wind blew across the ridge. Despite the exertion of their quicker pace, Weyr shivered.

They reached the end of the ridge. Weyr stopped. The ground sloped down toward another area thick with underbrush. Weyr looked for an opening or the hint of a trail but could not find one. He told Kamlar.

"We'll just have to cut into the woods," Weyr said.

"Do you have any idea where we're headed?"

"No. I wish I could look at the stars. At least that way we'd know which direction we're going."

"You can't see that far? Above the clouds?"

"I don't know. I never tried."

Weyr concentrated his sight upward into the clouds above them. All he saw was gray mist. The effort made him tired. He felt a dull pain at the base of his skull.

"It won't work. I can't get beyond the clouds," Weyr said.

"How far can you see on the ground?"

Weyr moved his sight horizontally as far as he could. At some distance — Weyr did not know how far — the images became blurred and distorted.

"A ways, but not too far," Weyr said. "All I can see are more hills. We'll just have to go on."

Kamlar gripped Weyr's shoulders from behind again, and they started down single file into the dense undergrowth. Weyr tried to pick the easiest way. He looked a few feet ahead of them, searched around rocks and behind trees to find openings in the brush, and then moved through them. But movement was slow and difficult. Thorny branches scratched their hands and faces.

The dull pain at the base of Weyr's skull increased. His shoulders ached from Kamlar's constant grip on them. It was hard to estimate time as they walked. Weyr thought it had been an hour or two since they had left the top of the hill when they stopped again to rest.

"Are we getting anywhere?" Kamlar said.

"I hope we're getting farther and farther away from Jocarra — and Faran."

"Are you sure we're not just going in circles?"

"How can I be sure?" Weyr snapped. The headache was making him irritable.

"I just asked," Kamlar said apologetically.

"I know. I'm sorry. My head hurts. I don't think we're going in circles. I haven't seen anything that looks familiar. But it's hard to tell in these deep woods."

They moved on. After what Weyr thought was another hour of walking through underbrush, they emerged onto a narrow rock ledge. Weyr peered over the edge. The ground sloped away very steeply. Alone, Weyr thought, he might have been able to negotiate the slope. There was no way he could guide Kamlar downward. Above them the ground rose sharply. They could not go up, either.

"There's a ledge here," Weyr said. "We'll have to go along it. Hold on tight."

The pain at the base of Weyr's skull had spread upward and forward. His temples ached. He pressed his thumbs against them to ease the pain, but that did not help. The ledge followed an irregular pattern along the side of the hill. Some parts of the ledge were only a foot or two wide. Nowhere was it more than four or five feet wide. As Weyr picked a way along the narrow pathway, his sight blurred occasionally. Once it stopped completely. With only his eyes, he could see almost nothing. Kamlar bumped into him as he stopped.

"Weyr, what is it?"

"I can't see," Weyr said. "The special sight is gone."

"Will it come back?"

"I've never been able to use it even this much before. I don't know."

Weyr tried consciously to relax. He chanted his word silently to himself. After a moment, the sight came back, but it was erratic, sometimes clear, sometimes blurred. His head hurt all over now. His legs ached. It was harder and harder to concentrate.

Abruptly the sight blacked out again. Weyr took a step and felt his foot slide on a loose rock. He lurched sideways toward the rim of the ledge. Kamlar's fingers bit into his shoulders. Weyr threw out his arms to try to regain his balance. He could not. He felt himself falling. His shoulder hit hard on the ground. He began to roll over and over down the rocky slope.

Weyr lost consciousness for a minute. When he came awake, he had stopped rolling. Something rough scratched his face. He put out a hand. Bark. He was wedged against a small tree trunk. Weyr sat up with his back to the tree. The shoulder he had hit when he fell hurt. He moved it. It did not seem to be broken. His legs and arms hurt, too. His head still ached.

"Kam?" Weyr said softly. "Kam, where are you?"

There was no answer.

"Kam!" Weyr said, louder. "Are you there, Kam?"

Weyr heard a moan.

"Kam, is that you?"

"I'm here, Weyr." Kamlar's voice sounded near. "Can you see me?"

"I can't see much of anything," Weyr said. He glanced upward. He could barely make out the branches of the tree above him. "The special sight is completely gone, now. I can't see any more than you can. Can you see me?"

"No."

"We can't be too far apart if we can hear each other so easily," Weyr said. "Can you come over here?"

"I'll try. I . . . ow!" Kamlar moaned again. "Ab splatter!"

"What's wrong?"

"My ankle. I must have twisted it when I fell. I think it's either sprained or broken. I can't walk."

"I'll try to come to you," Weyr said. "Keep talking, so I can hear where you are."

"All right. Come on, Weyr. I'm over here. Come over here. . . ."

As Kamlar chanted, Weyr stood. Leaning in order to keep his balance on the steep slope, he began to half walk, half crawl among the rocks and shrubs toward Kamlar's voice. Stones slipped away beneath his feet. By the sound of them, they seemed to roll a little way and then, after a moment, hit something with a sharp ping. Twice Weyr stumbled and fell. Kamlar's voice grew louder. At last Weyr saw a dim outline of the other boy just above him.

"I'm here. Give me a hand, Kam," Weyr said.

The feel of Kamlar's hand in his was welcome. Weyr pulled himself up and sat beside him. Kamlar's outline was a faint silhouette.

"What happened up there?" Kamlar said.

"All of a sudden the sight just gave out. I couldn't use it at all."

"It's gone now, too?"

"Yes. My head hurts when I try to use it. It pretty much hurts anyway," Weyr said. He rubbed the base of his skull, but the throb did not abate. "How's your ankle?"

"It hurts, too. But there's not much we can do about that if we can't see anything."

"What happens if Jocarra and her bunch come after us?" Weyr said.

"I doubt that they'll come in the dark," Kamlar said. "These hills are pretty rough. I don't think they could see much, even with torches. The morning is something else."

"We've put a good distance between us and them," Weyr said. "I hope."

"I hope, too," Kamlar said. "It's sure we can't go on now."

"I guess we'll just have to stay here for the night," Weyr said. "In the morning we should be able to see in the regular way."

Weyr felt a gust of cold wind tug at his jacket and pulled the garment around him. He stared into the darkness for a moment. An absurd thought struck him.

"You can't walk and neither of us can see," Weyr said. "I guess that's what we get for going out into the woods."

"What?" Kamlar said.

"There are lots of trees and bare roots and rocks in the woods. It's easy to slip on them," Weyr said.

Kamlar was silent for a moment. Then he laughed.

"Some slips," Kamlar said.

"Slips like nobody ever had before," Weyr said.

"Nobody. Ever," Kamlar said.

Sitting side by side on the rocky slope, they both laughed. As the night grew colder, they huddled together against the chill of the wind. Weyr's head nodded drowsily. It was good to feel the warmth of Kamlar's body near him. It had been good to laugh, too. Weyr again heard a wolf howl in the distance.

~

Dawn came without sun. Clouds still covered the sky. In the dim light Weyr could see a row of trees silhouetted against gray sky on a hill across from him. Directly below him, the slope on which he and Kamlar sat ended abruptly. Weyr saw the tops of a few trees beyond.

Kamlar's arm was around Weyr's shoulder. The other

boy was dozing, as Weyr realized he himself had done off and on during the night, despite the cold. Weyr disengaged himself gently so he would not wake Kamlar and walked cautiously down the slope. His muscles felt stiff and his skin throbbed from many scratches, but the headache he had had the night before was gone. Perhaps fifteen yards down, the slope ended in a cliff. Weyr looked over. A sheer rock wall dropped straight down to the boulder-strewn bed of a stream a good distance below. Peering over the cliff set Weyr's teeth on edge.

"What are you looking at, Weyr?" Kamlar said behind him.

"There's a cliff here," Weyr said as he climbed back up to Kamlar. "It must be sixty, seventy feet straight down. If we'd rolled another few feet, we'd have been gone."

Kamlar gave a low whistle.

"How's your ankle?" Weyr said when he reached Kamlar.

"It feels stiff. And it's still swollen. Look." Kamlar untied the band at the base of his trouser leg, pulled the cloth up, and loosened his boot. His ankle was puffy and discolored. "I can move it some, though."

"Do you think you can walk on it?"

"I don't know. We should bind it up."

"I'll use my blav."

Kamlar did not object. Weyr removed his jacket and peeled off his shirt. He felt goose bumps on his back and arms. Weyr quickly put his jacket back on. It was torn in several places from the fall, and the rough wool prickled against his arms, but it was warm.

Weyr took a sharp rock, cut into his blav with it, and

began to tear the shirt into strips. In a few minutes he had made a rough bandage, which he tied over the sole of Kamlar's boot and around his ankle. He helped Kamlar stand. Kamlar took a few short steps, leaning on Weyr. He winced.

"How does it feel?" Weyr said.

"I can walk on it," Kamlar said. His face looked more pale than usual. "But I won't be able to go very fast. Where do we go?"

"Back up to the ledge, I guess," Weyr said. "We can't very well go down. *That* would be some slip."

Kamlar snorted.

The ledge was perhaps thirty feet above them. They crawled up on their hands and knees. Near the top, Kamlar found a sturdy straight branch to use as a walking stick. They reached the ledge and stood up. The ledge was too narrow for them to walk side by side.

"Which way?" Weyr said. The ground above the ledge sloped sharply upward. He pointed backward. "We came from there."

"Then let's go on the other way," Kamlar said. "You thought we were getting away from Jocarra. We may come on something."

"Like what?"

"There are people who live up here, sheep herders, hunters, and such, Mountain Tam. Maybe if we're lucky, we'll hit one of their settlements."

"Would they help us?"

"I don't know. Mountain Tam aren't supposed to like the Agari too much. But people say they're friendly when they meet someone who's in trouble. And you're Tam. That might help. What else can we look for?"

"I don't know."

"I wish the sun was out," Kamlar said. "At least that way we could tell which direction we're going. It'd make us less likely to go in circles once we get off this ledge. Can you see anything with that funny sight of yours?"

Weyr reached out. For a moment he saw the part of the ledge that lay just beyond a curve, but the picture was blurred. The image faded. There was a dull throb at the base of his skull again.

"Not much," Weyr said.

"Maybe it'll come back," Kamlar said. "At least we can both see in the regular way now."

They started along the ledge. Kamlar, with his walking stick, hobbled ahead of Weyr so that Weyr could see and help him if he stumbled. Weyr heard Kamlar suck in his breath from time to time when his injured ankle twisted unexpectedly on a loose rock, but the boy said nothing. The ledge wound and turned around the mountain. There were no breaks in the sharp slope above it. Below them Weyr could still pick out the edge of the cliff.

The ledge seemed endless, but Weyr realized that the feeling came mostly from the slow progress they made because of Kamlar's injured ankle. Walking made Weyr warmer. He wiped sweat from his brow with the torn sleeve of his jacket.

As they walked, Weyr tried out his extended sight several times. Each time he could see a little farther and a little more clearly, but the sensations did not last. Once he heard a crash in the distance, like the sound of a large animal moving through underbrush. A question to Kamlar, who had not heard the noise, confirmed that Weyr had heard it with his extended senses. Like the sight, the hearing lasted for only a short time.

The next time they stopped to rest, Weyr heard distant sounds again.

"Listen," Weyr said.

"What?" Kamlar said.

"Voices," Weyr said. "I can hear voices. Can you hear them?"

"No," Kamlar said.

"It's my special hearing, then. There are people not far away."

"I told you there were settlements of Mountain Tam up here in the Hills. What are they saying? Can you understand them?"

"Wait," Weyr said.

Weyr concentrated on the voices and they became clearer. He felt his heart thump.

"It's Jocarra," Weyr said. "Jocarra and some man."

Chapter Nineteen

"WHERE ARE THEY?" Kamlar said, his voice a whisper.

"I can't tell for sure," Weyr said. He whispered, too. "They're close. I don't think I can usually hear very far that way."

"Can you see them?"

Fear knotted Weyr's stomach. With a surge of energy, his extended sight returned full force. Almost without effort, Weyr moved his inner eyes in the direction of the voices. He saw two figures silhouetted against the side of a hill.

"They're on this ledge, behind us," Weyr said.

"How far behind?"

Weyr saw Jocarra's slim figure ease off the ledge and move cautiously down the slope beside it. When she returned to the ledge, she carried a ragged piece of brightly colored cloth in her left hand. A heavily built Tamish man waited for her.

"Faran's with her," Weyr said. "They're back where we

fell off the ledge and had to stay the night. I ripped my jacket there. I remember now. Jocarra's found a piece of the jacket."

"Ab splatter!" Kamlar said.

"We can't have come too far from there," Weyr said.

"How much longer does this ledge go on?" Kamlar said.

Weyr brought his senses back to the spot where he and Kamlar stood. He moved his sight in widening circles around them. Above the ledge, the ground sloped up sharply as far as he could see. Below them, the steep drop ended in a cliff as it had ever since they had started to walk beside it that morning. Weyr followed the ledge in front of them until his vision blurred.

"It goes on as far as I can see," Weyr said.

"Now that they've seen that piece of jacket, they know we were there," Kamlar said. "They'll figure we're near, and they'll come on. I can't move very fast, that's for sure. Are they coming?"

Weyr extended his senses behind them. He saw Jocarra and Faran. They walked quickly along the ledge. An outcropping of rock above them looked familiar. He and Kamlar had passed it not too many minutes earlier.

"They're coming," Weyr said. "We can't get far with your leg. We certainly can't climb up. And the cliff's down below. We've got to find some place to hide or they'll trap us."

"Caves!" Kamlar said.

"What?"

"Caves. I told you, this whole area is honeycombed with

caves. Look, Weyr! Look with your funny sight. Find us a cave!"

Weyr again began to move his inner eyes in circles, looking along the ledge, above and below it, until he had reached the limit of his vision. He saw nothing that looked like the entrance to a cave.

"I can't see anything," Weyr said. He fought back panic. "No cave."

"Maybe there's one that's hidden — covered up or something," Kamlar said. "Look, Weyr, look!"

As Weyr began to move his inner eyes again, he felt a strange sensation. It was as though something was opening up inside his head. His extended sight was there, but so was another feeling. Weyr had an odd new sense of touch. Somehow he not only saw the ground around him. He felt it as well.

The tips of Weyr's fingers tingled. Without moving the fingers, he began to feel around him in wider and wider circles. He felt leaves, earth, rocks, tree roots, even an occasional scurrying insect. The new sense moved as rapidly as his inner eyes could move. It was as though his fingers had grown enormous and could cover huge areas in an instant, could feel the texture and contours of the ground as easily as his real hand might feel the texture and contours in a piece of cloth. His fingers, Weyr thought, were crawling — no, running — over the ground.

Weyr explored with the new sense, round and round, groping, feeling, touching. After a minute his mental touch located an opening in the ground. Weyr concentrated on it. Tangled branches covered the opening. Weyr felt through and beyond them. The space behind the branches was hollow. Weyr mentally spread his fingers. He touched stone walls. It was a cave.

"I found one!" Weyr said. "I found a cave. I didn't see it. I *touched* it, like I was feeling it with my hands."

"However you found it, you found it," Kamlar said. "Where is it, Weyr?"

"Above the ledge, a little farther on."

"Let's go! Tell me where to stop," Kamlar said.

Kamlar hobbled along the ledge. His breath hissed with each step. Weyr followed. They rounded a turn in the ledge.

"Up there," Weyr said. He pointed. "Maybe twenty, twenty-five feet up."

The hill sloped sharply. Roots of small trees clung to the crevices on the rocky slope. The entrance to the cave was completely hidden to Weyr's eyes, but he could feel it with his new touch.

"I can't see anything. I hope you're right," Kamlar said.

"I'm right," Weyr said. "Can you climb?"

"I can do whatever I have to," Kamlar said. "You go first. You can see the cave, or do whatever you're doing to find it. I'll follow you."

Weyr scrambled up the slope. He grasped tree roots and outcroppings of rock, searching for places to put his feet. Loose stones slipped away beneath him and rattled downward. He looked backward. Kamlar's face was set in a grimace of pain, but he made no sound except for the harsh wheeze of his breath between his teeth.

Weyr felt the entrance to the cave just above him. He crawled up, pushed the tangled branches aside, flung himself into the cave and turned to grab Kamlar's hand. The other boy came up beside him, breathing hard. Weyr pulled the branches back across the opening and settled onto his haunches. His breath came in short gasps. Light flickered through the branches. Weyr's right hand hurt. He looked at it. The palm was bleeding. Weyr sucked at it. The blood tasted salty. He heard Kamlar's labored breathing gradually begin to subside. Weyr looked around with his normal sight. The cave was small, barely big enough for both of them to fit into. But it would do.

A few minutes later Weyr heard two sets of footsteps on the ledge, one light, one heavy, heard them with his ears, not his extended hearing. His strange new sense of touch seemed to have receded, but his sight was still sharp. Without moving, Weyr peered out through the branches that covered the entrance to the cave.

Jocarra came around the bend in the ledge. Her step was light and nervous. Faran was just behind her. His legs were slightly bowed, and he walked with a heavy, awkward gait. Jocarra's and Faran's heads bobbed up and down as they scanned the area around them. They passed beneath the cave. Jocarra seemed to look directly at Weyr for a moment, but she did not stop. She and Faran walked on along the ledge and turned around another bend. Weyr watched them until they were perhaps fifty yards farther down the ledge and withdrew his extended sight.

Weyr let his breath go in a soft sigh. He had not realized he had been holding it.

"They're gone. Faran and Jocarra went by us. And they didn't see anything," Weyr said. "We're safe, Kam."

~

"It's witchcraft. I still say that," Weyr heard Faran's voice say a few moments later.

Weyr started. He reached out again to see Jocarra and Faran. They had stopped to rest perhaps two hundred yards farther along the ledge.

"Ab splatter!" Weyr heard Jocarra reply. "It's that kind of talk that makes Tam afraid of the Agari."

"Because you don't believe it doesn't mean it's not true," Faran said. "You told me Terif tied the Instrument's brat."

"He did."

"Then how did he and his tame Tam get free?"

"I don't know. Perhaps Terif wasn't as careful with the knots as he usually is. We know they used the metal plates to pry the bar off the door. It was a major mistake to leave them alone there. I'll take responsibility for that."

"Even so, how did they come so far, and at night? It was black as the Seventh Level of Torment last night. We know they came this far. You found that patch of cloth. There are a thousand places where they could have fallen, even in daylight. The Agari brat must be able to see in the dark."

"No one can see in the dark," Jocarra said. "They must have been incredibly lucky."

"I've heard stories about Agari who can see in the dark," Faran said, his voice nervous. "And about Agari who can do other witchcraft. People who can move things without touching them. They say some can even listen to other people's thoughts. Agari witches, they all are."

"Calling the Agari 'witches' sometimes has its uses, but I don't believe those stories about the Agari," Jocarra said in her staccato rhythms. "Furthermore, I've heard stories like that about Tam. Stories told by Agari. My family's Agari 'friends' talked that way sometimes when I was younger and had to spend time with them. I don't believe them, either."

"Then how did the Agari brat escape?"

"I don't know. It wasn't witchcraft," Jocarra said. She turned her head. "Faran, is that the others on the ridge across there?"

"I think so. Yes. It's Terif."

"Signal them, Faran," Jocarra said. "Get them over here. We're more likely to find the Instrument's whelp on this side of the valley."

Faran raised his voice in a howl that sounded like some animal Weyr could not identify. After a moment there was an answering howl from the other side of the valley.

"They'll come," Faran said. "It'll take them some time."

"And while they're coming, we'll keep looking. The Agari brat's luck can't hold forever," Jocarra said.

Weyr withdrew his extended senses.

"We're going to have to stay here for a while," Weyr told Kamlar. "Jocarra just signaled to bring some others over to this side of the valley. They're sure we're around. I think we'll be safe here, though, if we don't move."

"How long will we have to stay?" Kamlar said.

"I don't know. Probably until night again. Then maybe we can move on. Like you said, they can't search at night. But we can see at night. I can. I hope."

"I hope, too."

Weyr felt tension drain from his muscles. The base of

his skull ached again, though not as badly as it had the night before. Kamlar looked exhausted. His face was unusually pale.

"We should rest, Kam," Weyr said. "Especially you, with your ankle. We'll need all our strength if we're going out at night again."

"I know."

Within a few minutes Kamlar was asleep. He snored slightly. The cave was warm and comfortable. There were things he should think about, Weyr knew, but the warmth of the cave made him drowsy. Weyr slept, too.

Chapter Twenty

IT WAS STILL light when Weyr woke, though the gray sky that showed through the branches at the mouth of the cave made it difficult to tell how long he had slept. Weyr was hungry, and his mouth was dry from thirst, but he felt somewhat rested. The headache was gone.

Weyr extended his sight in widening circles. Just at the edge of his range of vision he saw Terif and a woman he did not know searching near the ledge where he and Kamlar had spent the night. Weyr sighed in relief. He and Kamlar were still safe.

Weyr looked at Kamlar. He was still asleep. Weyr smiled at the sleeping boy. Kamlar was his friend. He trusted Kamlar, Weyr realized, trusted him more than he had ever trusted anyone.

And that felt good.

"Are you using your funny sight to check on Faran and Jocarra, Weyr?" Kamlar said as he opened his eyes.

Kamlar yawned. His cheeks were not as pale as they had been earlier.

"They're still looking for us," Weyr said. "But they're not anywhere near."

"Good," Kamlar said. He rubbed his eyes. "That was some luck that you found this cave. No, not luck, I guess. But it sure saved our hides."

Kamlar rubbed absently at his sore ankle. He tilted his head. His eyes looked puzzled.

"Weyr, can I ask you something?" Kamlar said.

"Of course," Weyr said.

"Why did you say you were responsible for us being caught?" Kamlar said.

Weyr paused. "That afternoon I saw and heard Faran — I didn't know it was him, of course — and some others talking about your father," he said. "And then later I saw them move down the hill toward your father. Saw and heard them with my special sight and hearing, I mean." Weyr paused again. "I . . . I was pretty sure they were going to do something."

"I remember. You told me you heard them. I couldn't figure out how you could have heard anybody out in front there," Kamlar said. He grinned. "Now I know."

"I should have warned the guards," Weyr said miserably. His guilt returned to him in a burst.

"There wouldn't have been much time," Kamlar said.

"Still, I should have tried," Weyr said.

"Why didn't you?" There was no accusation in Kamlar's voice, only a gentle question. "Don't tell me if it's none of my affair."

"I don't mind talking about it. You're the first person I've told about all this for a long time. I . . . I made a rule for myself," Weyr said slowly. "That I would never tell anyone about the special sight and hearing. Never."

"Why?"

"When I was younger, I told some people about . . . about what I could do. I told Gran. She beat me for it," Weyr said. "And I told some other people in Bown. Mostly I told children, but the adults found out about it, too. People started to call me witch behind my back. Sometimes they called me that to my face. Only . . . only they didn't say it like you said it when you asked me if I was a witch. They hated me for it." The memory brought Weyr close to tears. "Relinda says people hate you if you're different."

"I don't hate you for it," Kamlar said. "I don't understand it, but I don't hate you for it."

"I know."

"I couldn't hate you for it, Weyr. Or for anything else I could think of," Kamlar said. "And I don't think you ought to feel responsible for us getting kidnapped. It all happened so fast. How could you have warned anybody? And if you had, who would have believed you? I didn't. I wouldn't have believed any of it until after what you did last night and today. I can hardly believe it now. It's not your fault that Jocarra and her bunch did what they did. And anyway, you're the one that got us away from them."

"I guess that's all true," Weyr said. He was not altogether convinced of what Kamlar had said. But some of the guilt he had felt was gone. "That makes me feel a little better, Kam."

They were silent for a moment. A light breeze rustled

the branches over the mouth of the cave. Weyr shifted his weight slightly. His muscles still felt cramped.

"Did Faran or Jocarra say anything about what they were going to do?" Kamlar asked.

"No," Weyr said. "But they said some other things." He described to Kamlar the conversation he had overheard about stories of witchcraft among both Agari and Tam. "You said the same thing, too, didn't you, Kam? What kind of stories have you heard?"

"It was a little ridiculous for me to say that," Kamlar said. His face flushed pink. "I guess a lot of the stories were just tales for children. Some Agari — at least those back in the mountains, near Elubin — make Tam out to be, well, like monsters. Adults use Tam to scare children, to make them do as they're told. They say 'The Tam witches will get you if you're not good,' that kind of thing."

"In Bown adults did the same thing with tales about Agari," Weyr said. "My gran used to tell me things like that. What are Tamish witches supposed to be able to do?"

"In the stories, they're able to see things no one else can see — I guess you can really do that, can't you? — and to move things without touching them. Some of them are supposed to be able to fly." Kamlar's eyebrows shot up. "Can *you* fly, Weyr?"

Weyr snorted. "Not that I know of," he said. "I wish I could. I'd fly us out of here. If there are witches like that, I'm certainly not one of them."

Kamlar laughed. "More's the pity," he said. "Anyway, most people who know anything don't take those stories too seriously." He eyed Weyr curiously. "Now I guess I think they should. The stories about seeing things no one else can, anyway. Maybe that's why my father . . ."

Kamlar stopped short. His blue eyes looked very troubled. He sat silent for a long moment.

"You should never, ever, tell my father about what you can do, Weyr," Kamlar said at last. His voice was low and serious. "Never."

Weyr blinked, startled at Kamlar's sudden intensity.

"Why not?" Weyr said. "Because he'll think I'm a witch?"

"No. Because he won't."

"What do you mean?"

"I . . . I should have thought of this before," Kamlar said slowly. "I was too upset and scared to think straight."

"Thought of what?"

"Lately — just in the last couple of years or so — my father has gotten interested in stories about people who can do funny things, the kind of things you can do. Tam stories and Agari stories, both. He more or less collects those stories. And I'm sure he doesn't believe they have anything to do with witchcraft. I haven't paid too much attention. He gets interested in unusual subjects, sometimes, my father. And anyhow he doesn't speak much to me about the stories. But I've heard him talk with his friends about them."

"What does he say?"

"He says he wants information. He wants to meet someone who can do those things."

"Why shouldn't I tell him about what I can do?"

"Because if he knows what you can do, my father will find a way to use you," Kamlar said.

"Use me?" Weyr said.

"Yes. Use you. My father uses people." Kamlar twisted his hands together nervously. "My father's a powerful man. And he uses people — controls them — for his political work. I guess it's part of his job. If he finds someone who can do something, has a skill or a talent of some kind, he tries to get them to work for him. Not for him, he says, but 'for the good of the cause' — so that Tam and Agari don't have the wars they used to, and their merchants can trade with one another in peace. That's how he uses people." Kamlar's pale cheeks flushed. "My father wouldn't like to hear me say that about him. But it's true. If he knew about your funny sight and hearing, he'd try to use them, try to do that with you." Kamlar's face twisted in a grimace. "Sometimes he uses me that way — for his politics."

Kamlar's voice had a bitter tone Weyr had never heard before. Kamlar swallowed hard and looked down at his hands. When he looked back at Weyr, his eyes were moist.

"I . . . I don't want to say any more about that," Kamlar said. His voice was not quite steady. "Maybe I shouldn't have said it at all. But I had to. You mustn't tell my father about your funny sight and all. And Weyr, I promise, if we get out of here and back to Domn, I'll never tell anyone about what you can do. Not unless you want me to. And especially I won't tell my father."

For a moment Weyr was too surprised at what Kamlar had said to speak. And yet, he realized, some part of him was not surprised at all. The Instrument was a striking figure. Weyr had been impressed, even intimidated, by him. But though he had never before said it to himself, Weyr knew that he did not fully trust the Instrument.

What Kamlar had said also made him feel relieved. He had not really considered what Kamlar might do with the information he now had about the extended senses. But in some corner of his mind, Weyr recognized, he had had a nagging fear about it. The fear was gone.

"Thank you for that, Kam," Weyr said at last. "I know I can trust you."

"You can trust me," Kamlar said. He looked directly at Weyr. His blue eyes were still moist. "You're the best friend I've ever had, Weyr."

Weyr felt suddenly shy. He smiled at Kamlar.

"You're the only real friend I've ever had, Kam," Weyr said. "But I couldn't imagine a better one."

~

He had been right when he predicted that Jocarra and Faran would not try to search for them at night. Periodically after his talk with Kamlar, Weyr extended his sight and hearing to search for them. They were never close to the cave. An hour or so later, when the light had grown dim, Weyr heard Jocarra give a disgusted command ordering all of her party to return to their camp. As darkness fell, Weyr looked as far as he could with his senses. He could find no trace of the Tamish searchers.

Weyr and Kamlar emerged from their cave and half slid, half crawled to the ledge below. Weyr stood up and stretched his cramped muscles. Kamlar did the same, then lifted his foot and moved it in a circle.

"My ankle's better," Kamlar said. "The rest did it good. I can walk again. At least if we don't go too fast."

"Let me know if it bothers you," Weyr said.

"Right."

Clouds still covered the sky. Weyr could see virtually nothing with his regular eyes, but with his inner eyes he could see as if it was daylight. His head no longer ached.

"Let's go," Weyr said.

They started single file along the ledge again. After a time, the ledge widened and they could walk side by side. Weyr spied a spring bubbling out from under a rock. The water was cold and delicious. Both boys drank eagerly.

Finally the ledge ended in a hill that sloped down into another wooded area. The vegetation in the area was thinner than it had been in the woods they had traveled the day before. There were occasional clearings in the trees.

When they stopped in the first clearing, Weyr looked up and saw stars. The clouds had broken. For a moment he was afraid. If he could see normally, so could Jocarra and Faran. But they had put a good distance between them and the cave on the ledge. And he had heard Jocarra give the command to return to camp.

"There's the Waterfall," Weyr said. "At least we'll know which direction we're moving. We can keep from circling."

"What direction should we take?" Kamlar said.

"Who knows? Pick a direction."

"East," Kamlar said.

"East it is," Weyr said.

Movement was easier for Kamlar as dim starlight filtered through the trees. A few minutes later, Sprite rose. With the moonlight, Kamlar found a waist-high bush filled with purple berries the size of Weyr's thumbnail.

"Hungry?" Kamlar said.

"Starved."

"Try these." Kamlar held a handful of berries out to Weyr. "I can't remember what my father called them, but I know they're safe to eat."

The purple berries were slightly sour, but the flavor was not unpleasant.

"I'm sorry they're not Agari Fire, Weyr," Kamlar said. "I know you miss that."

Weyr laughed. "Actually, I do miss it," he said. "But these will do fine until I can get back to it."

They ate their fill before they again moved eastward.

Each time they entered a clearing and checked their direction with the stars, Weyr scanned as far as he could in an effort to pick out the easiest path. It seemed to him that each time he could see farther and farther ahead. At last, he scanned from a clearing and his heart leaped.

"Kam," Weyr said. "Kam! I can see a road. A real road! And it looks like a big one."

"Breath of Life," Kamlar said. "Sweet, sweet Breath of Life. Can you take us there?"

"Yes," Weyr said. "I can. I know I can."

Chapter Twenty-One

THEY REACHED THE road just after sunrise. Kamlar was sure it was part of The Great Way, but as a precaution he and Weyr decided to hide in the shrubbery beside the road to see who passed. There were no early-morning travelers for several minutes.

"What are you going to tell your father?" Weyr said as they waited.

"I've been thinking about that," Kamlar said. "I've made up a story."

"Like the story we told about the time we fought in the woods?" Weyr said.

Kamlar laughed. Then his face turned somber.

"No. Better than that. This is serious. We simply can't let my father know what you can do with your sight and hearing," Kamlar said. The corners of his mouth turned up in an ironic half smile. "Actually, I'm going to use some advice my father gave me about lying."

"What's that?"

"He said once that if you think something is important

enough to tell a lie about, then it's important enough to
tell a good lie. And a good lie should stay as close to the
truth as possible. That way it's more convincing, and also
you aren't so likely to get confused when you say it. So I'm
going to tell my father you rescued me."

"I think we rescued each other," Weyr said. "You
were the one who knew about the country and the
caves."

"Maybe a little," Kamlar said. "But you're the one who
got us out. And I want my father to know that. I'm going
to tell him the story as much like the way it really happened
as I can. We were tied up, but you figured out a way to
untie us — maybe Terif was careless with the knots — and
we used the plates to open the door."

"It was dark then."

"My father doesn't know that. Who'll tell him, Jocarra?"
Weyr laughed.

"I'll tell the truth about the next part of the story —
how I hurt my ankle and we spent the night outdoors.
Then, in the morning, you saw Faran and Jocarra off in
the distance searching for us, and you found a cave for us
to hide in."

"How did I do that?"

"I heard Nomer tell my father once that you have very
sharp eyes. So you saw Faran and Jocarra and found the
cave with your sharp eyes. We hid there until dark. And
later, in the moonlight, with your sharp eyes you found a
. . . let's see . . . a small brook and we followed the bed of
it down to The Great Way."

"Some story," Weyr said.

Kamlar smiled wryly. "When my father gave me that

advice about lying, I doubt he thought I'd use it with him."

"Have you ever lied that way to your father before?" Weyr said.

"Not about anything that mattered," Kamlar said. He looked at Weyr. His blue eyes shone bright in the morning sun. "This matters."

"Will your father believe you?"

"I'll make him believe me," Kamlar said.

~

A few moments later Weyr heard horses.

"Someone's coming," Weyr said.

Weyr and Kamlar peered out through a break in the shrubs. Four of the Instrument's guards rode slowly along the road. One was Valmo. The guards looked ragged and weary.

When Weyr and Kamlar stepped out onto the road, the guards reined up their horses and stared silently at them for a moment. Then they all began to talk loudly at once. Weyr could understand only some of the words, but he heard one guard's voice clearly.

"Praise to all The Powers," the guard said. "It's the Instrument's son."

~

The next few minutes were a blur of noise and motion. Kamlar and the guards chattered to one another in Agari too rapid for Weyr to understand. At first the guards ignored Weyr. Then Kamlar pointed at him and talked earnestly in Agari. The guards whooped and laughed and clapped Weyr on the back. One of Valmo's claps almost knocked him off his feet. Surprised and embarrassed, Weyr grinned sheepishly at the Agari men.

"They're congratulating you, Weyr. I told them how you rescued me. That is," Kamlar added in a low tone, "I told them some of my story of it."

Valmo cut away the crude bandage Weyr had tied around Kamlar's foot, took off his boot, and examined his ankle. Weyr saw tears on Valmo's cheeks. With a flash of sympathy, Weyr realized that Valmo, too, probably felt responsible for their capture.

A guard produced a skin of water and a cloth so Valmo could clean Kamlar's ankle. Another brought large leaves that held cold tofer. The highly spiced dish tasted delicious. Weyr ate greedily.

"Valmo doesn't think my ankle's broken," Kamlar said after a few moments. The guard began to tie up his foot with a clean roll of cloth. "It's probably only a bad sprain."

A guard helped Kamlar up onto one of the horses and eased into the saddle behind him. Valmo and another guard talked loudly with one another. Weyr heard his name mentioned. Both guards pointed in his direction.

"They're arguing about who gets the honor of having you ride with him, Weyr," Kamlar said.

"Valmo," Weyr said without hesitation.

Valmo beamed as though he had been given a great gift, grabbed Weyr around the waist, swung him up atop his horse as if he weighed almost nothing, and then mounted in front of Weyr.

"My father has set up a headquarters camp up the road a ways," Kamlar said. "We'll go there."

The guards set off at a canter, but at a command from Kamlar they slowed to a more leisurely pace. As they rode, Kamlar plied the guards with questions. Gradually, from Kamlar's translations and Valmo's halting Tam, Weyr pieced together the story of what had happened after he and Kamlar had been kidnapped.

The Instrument's guards had tried to capture Faran, but the press of the audience and standing orders not to attack unarmed Tam had made it difficult for them to move. In the midst of the turmoil, a guard who had remained at the nearby Agari camp rushed to the amphitheatre to announce that there was a fire in the camp.

"The fire was what Jocarra meant when she talked about a 'secondary diversion,'" Kamlar said. "Some others of her bunch must have set it. What with the crowd and the fire, Faran just slipped away." He frowned. "Very, very clever. They really knew what they were doing."

The Instrument, the guards said, had been frantic with worry when he had discovered that Kamlar and Weyr were gone. He had set the guards searching the immediate area, but without success. Soon he hired men and women in Warn to join the search. At the same time, a fast-riding guard with an extra horse was dispatched to Domn to bring more people to help. The man made the two-day ride to Domn overnight. The first contingent from Domn arrived late the next afternoon. The next day more people from Domn arrived. The Hills brimmed with searchers. There were several hundred, the guards thought.

The more Weyr heard of the guards' stories, the more amazed he became. He had gotten somewhat used to the idea that he was "under the Instrument's protection."

Now, Weyr realized, he had had no idea of what the phrase might actually mean.

It was true that the Instrument's "protection" had not kept them from being kidnapped. Nor had it rescued them. The Instrument must have known that he had little chance of finding Kamlar. But still, in two days' time, the Instrument had brought in several hundred people to search for them. That was more people than — according to Gran's carefully kept records — lived in the whole village of Bown, if you counted every woman, man, and child.

Kamlar did not seem even a little surprised that the Instrument had brought in so many searchers. But Weyr found the idea that one man could command so many people so quickly astonishing. Kamlar had said that the Instrument, when he could, used people. Weyr thought he was just beginning, a little, to understand what Kamlar meant.

~

The Instrument's headquarters camp was a disorderly collection of tents, horses, and wagons nestled into a small, flat area between two hills. Weyr saw Nomer and Relinda's brightly colored wagon among the others. Perhaps two or three dozen men and women moved in the area. Most of the searchers, Weyr realized, were still out looking for them.

As they rode into the camp, people clustered around them, shouting and waving. Above the clamor, Weyr heard the Instrument's commanding tenor. The cluster of people parted. Kamlar slid down from the guard's horse and ran into his father's arms. At first no one paid Weyr any attention. He eased off Valmo's horse.

"Weyr! Weyr! Sweet Breath of Life, you're safe!"

Relinda's low voice cut through the babble of the crowd. Weyr turned toward her. Relinda rushed up to him and hugged him, hard. She muttered unintelligible words against his ear. Weyr felt a tug at the leg of his tob and looked down. Berthin peeked up at him, her face somewhere between tears and laughter. With one hand Weyr ruffled Berthin's hair.

Huge hands gripped Weyr's shoulders and turned him around. He felt himself lifted off his feet, caught around the waist in Nomer's powerful arms.

Nomer clutched Weyr and spun him in a kind of wild dance. He set Weyr back on the ground and gripped him by the shoulders to hold him at arms' length and look at him. Nomer struggled to speak but could not. Tears streamed down his face. Relinda, too, was crying. His own eyes were wet, Weyr realized. Nomer hugged him again, then Relinda. Weyr could not remember ever being hugged as Nomer and Relinda hugged him. It felt good.

"Nomer! Relinda!" the Instrument's voice called from a few feet away. "Come over here. Bring the Tamish boy with you. We will go into my tent, where we can talk. It appears that I have your protégé to thank for my son's release, and quite possibly for his life."

~

"Faran and the others were in on it," Kamlar said. "But Jocarra was the one behind it. She was giving the orders."

"I know," the Instrument said. "A courier arrived from

Domn this morning with her demands and a note from you."

Kamlar and the Instrument were speaking in Tam for his benefit, Weyr knew. A cool breeze blew in through the open door of the Instrument's tent. Weyr realized that it was the first time he had ever been inside the tent. Tufted rugs with elaborate designs on them covered the dirt floor. A guard had brought wooden chairs with brightly colored cloth seats. Another guard served all of them — Nomer, Relinda, Berthin, the Instrument, Kamlar, and Weyr — steaming hamar in multicolored pottery mugs.

"What did Jocarra want, Father?" Kamlar said.

"Money." The Instrument's voice was harsh. There were dark hollows under his eyes. "A good deal of money. And some political concessions, the exact nature of which is a matter too complicated to explain. It was a vicious act to take you. And a cowardly act. I would have thought better of Jocarra, fanatic though she is. They must be desperate up there in the Hills, to use children as pieces in their game. Though they obviously did not reckon on the character of the children."

"They made me write that note," Kamlar said. He sounded contrite. Weyr remembered that Kamlar had somehow felt that he had betrayed his father. "I didn't want to write it, but I knew you'd be worried. I thought you'd want to know I was alive and . . ."

"Of course. You had no choice," the Instrument said. His voice softened. "What else did they do to you? Did they beat you? I want to hear the entire story."

"They didn't beat us," Kamlar said. "They tied us up

and locked us in a cave, but otherwise they didn't hurt us. They even fed us."

"If you were tied and locked in, how did you manage to get away?"

Kamlar shot Weyr a quick glance and began his story. The other boy, Weyr thought as Kamlar told the tale, was quite ably following his father's advice about lies. Most of what Kamlar said was true. He accurately described the cave where they had been imprisoned, their treatment by Jocarra, their escape using the plates to open the door, their wandering in the hills, their hiding place in the second cave. The invented parts of the story seemed to fit in naturally with the rest. The tale as a whole was most convincing, Weyr thought, even to him, and he knew which parts of it were truth and which were not. Altogether, Kamlar was a persuasive liar. In fact, it seemed to Weyr that Kamlar actually enjoyed telling the story.

Weyr was not entirely comfortable with the elaborate praise that Kamlar heaped on him for his role in their escape, but Kamlar had insisted that be part of the tale. Weyr glanced at the Instrument off and on during Kamlar's recitation. The Agari man listened closely and asked an occasional question, but for the most part he simply nodded as though the story made sense to him.

"So it was really Weyr who got us out," Kamlar concluded. "If it hadn't been for Weyr, I wouldn't be here at all."

"It seems that my son has been most fortunate in his choice of a friend," the Instrument said. He glanced at Nomer. "As I have been."

The Instrument rose and took a few steps to stand in

front of Weyr. Automatically, Weyr stood, too. With one hand, the Instrument vigorously shook Weyr's hand. With the other, he held Weyr's arm at the elbow. Weyr blinked in surprise. No one had ever shaken his hand like that. Among the Tam, only adults shook hands that way, Weyr knew, and then only in a very few formal or highly emotional situations. Weyr felt awkward as he gripped the Instrument in the same fashion.

"My boy, there are no words for my gratitude," the Instrument said. His voice was warm. Then he dropped Weyr's hand and arm, bowed deeply from the waist, and said in a formal tone, "Si'be Weyr, the service of the Instrument of the Merchants of Elubin is at your command."

Weyr blinked again. The Instrument had called him "si'be." No one called a child "si'be." And the phrase the Instrument had used was one of the most formal of Tamish utterances. It was a phrase used among equals. Adult equals. The Instrument was treating him as he would an adult to whom he owed a debt.

"It's all right. I don't want . . ." Weyr began. He felt blood rush to his face as he stumbled over his words. He took a deep breath. "I was just the lucky one. Kam would have got us loose if he could have. And it could just as well have been me that was injured. Kam would have done the same thing for me if it'd been me that got hurt."

"I respect my son enough to believe that would be true," the Instrument said. "Still, it was your courage that brought the matter to a successful conclusion." He turned to Kamlar. "Kam, have you anything to say to Weyr?"

"I've already said my thanks to Weyr, Father," Kamlar

said. The other boy bowed his head slightly at Weyr. He grinned. There was just a trace of mischief in the grin, Weyr thought. "I've said my thanks in the best way I know how."

"I'm sure you have," the Instrument said.

Weyr was sure Kamlar had, too.

"Excellent, excellent," the Instrument said. "And we will have, I hope, many more opportunities to express our gratitude to Weyr during the coming days in Domn. Si'be Weyr, I hope you will honor me by being a guest in my house for as long as you wish while you see to whatever affairs you need to conduct in Domn."

Again, the Instrument was talking to him as though he was an adult.

"I'd be . . . pleased to be your guest," Weyr said. He searched for something else to say. "Relinda told me Domn's a fine city."

"As always, Relinda exhibits exquisite taste," the Instrument said. "However, she understates. Domn is not simply a fine city. Domn is a *great* city. A great city of the Tamish people. With, if I may say so, a few dashes of Agari Fire to give it spice. I hope you'll find the combination congenial." The Instrument gave one of his hooting laughs. "I have often felt, Weyr, that you are a Tam who has a little bit of Agari in his heart."

Weyr heard Relinda suck in her breath. Her brown Tamish face wrinkled with concern. Weyr fingered his tattered Agari jacket. He glanced quickly at Nomer, at Berthin, at Kamlar, and then back at Relinda.

Weyr winked at Relinda. A smile broke over her face. She winked back.

Weyr turned to the Instrument.

"Thank you, si'be," Weyr said. "That's exactly how I feel."

~

"If my father doesn't stop fussing, we won't get home until the Third Level of Torment freezes over!" Kamlar said. "I swear he checked every hair on my head to make sure it was in its proper place."

Kamlar limped slightly as he led his dun horse up beside Weyr. He wore a blue blav and dark-blue trousers, both obviously made of fine material, and knee-length boots. Early-morning sunlight made the polished leather of the boots shine.

"You look elegant," Weyr said.

Kamlar snorted. "Be grateful Father doesn't think he can groom *you*," he said. "Come on. You're supposed to be in the place of honor, right behind the leads. Your horse is waiting for you up there."

Kamlar pointed. Weyr saw Nomer and Relinda's wagon near the front of a line of horses and wagons. There was a riderless horse just ahead of it. As he and Kamlar walked toward them, Weyr heard the Instrument's voice behind him, barking commands. The Instrument had been making inspections all morning.

"Why is your father paying so much attention to everyone's appearance?" Weyr said.

"More politics," Kamlar said in a slightly sarcastic tone. "We'll get into the hinterlands around Domn today. That's my father's territory. He wants to 'offer a proper representation of the Agari presence.'" Kamlar raised an eyebrow. "We probably do look impressive, at that."

On impulse, Weyr decided to see how the Agari party did, in fact, look. He sent his extended sight to a spot a hundred feet or so up a hill. As it had every time he had tried to use the sense since returning to the Instrument's camp, the sight came almost without effort. For a moment, Weyr marveled at that. Using his extended senses felt natural to him now, like using his regular eyes or ears. He could do what he wanted with them.

It was an exhilarating feeling.

Nomer had told him that the Instrument had dismissed all the searchers from Warn and had sent a number of the people who had come from Domn on ahead. Even so, Weyr thought, the Instrument's party had to number a hundred or more. It stretched along a substantial expanse beside The Great Way. In the sunlight, the colors of the Agari clothing seemed even brighter than usual. The lead guards carried banners emblazoned with a complicated geometric pattern. Weyr saw the Instrument wheeling his horse along the line of march.

"We do," Weyr said. He withdrew his extended sight. "We look very impressive."

"How do you know . . ." Kamlar began. He laughed. "Where were you?"

Weyr pointed. "Up there."

"You *are* something," Kamlar said.

"Maybe I should do your father's inspection for him," Weyr said. "I could cover the territory in no time. Then we could get going."

Kamlar laughed. "Don't think my father wouldn't have you do it, if he knew," he said.

"Then it's a good thing he doesn't."

Kamlar's voice turned serious. "And he never will," he said.

"I know," Weyr said. "Thanks, Kam."

~

Weyr briefly examined the fine black horse the Instrument had provided for him and then, while Kamlar chatted with a nearby guard, dropped back to greet Nomer, Relinda, and Berthin. The Instrument passed him, evidently on his way to the head of the line.

"Ho, Weyr," Nomer said. "By tomorrow night we'll be in Domn. Excited?"

"Am I!"

"Not any more than we are," Relinda said.

"I bet you'll be glad to see your cousin, Weyr," Berthin said.

Weyr started. He had all but forgotten he had told the lie about his cousin in Domn to Nomer, Relinda, and Berthin. Jocarra's harsh questions about the tale flickered in his mind.

"I guess I will," Weyr said uncertainly.

Relinda laid a hand on Berthin's shoulder. "What Weyr will do in Domn is his affair, Berth," Relinda said. "We're only glad we'll see a lot of him."

Weyr raised his eyebrows quizzically.

"The Instrument has invited us to be his guests, too, Weyr," Relinda said. "We'll be staying with him for a time."

"That's wonderful!" Weyr said. He hesitated a moment. "I . . . I don't really have a cousin in Domn, you know. That was just a story I made up so people wouldn't bother me."

Nomer nodded. "Rel and I figured so," he said.

"The truth is I don't have any family in Domn at all," Weyr said.

Nomer's hand swept out in a gesture that embraced Relinda, Berthin, Kamlar, and the Instrument.

"Well, then, Weyr," Nomer said, "I'm afraid you'll just have to make do with all of us."

Weyr swallowed hard to relieve the lump that seemed to have suddenly developed in his throat.

"I guess I can manage that," Weyr said.

~

"Forward!" The Instrument's tenor rang the command.

Weyr mounted his horse. He and Kamlar joined the line of march as it slowly began to move. Behind them, Nomer's resonant bass lined out the first phrase of a familiar Agari song. Relinda took up the chorus. Others joined in. So did Weyr. The music sounded good. Weyr heard Kamlar's tones, off-key as usual, and then the Instrument's drone. Even they sounded good.

Weyr sent his extended hearing to listen from a spot several yards up the hill above him. A hundred and more voices strong, the Instrument's party sang. The music rose toward a final chord. Weyr listened carefully until he picked out the notes he wanted to hear.

Among the voices, Weyr heard his own clear treble ring with sure and true harmony as the Agari music echoed up through the Hills of Karmon and along the road that led to Domn.